CHRONICLES

The Ratastrophe Catastrophe

THE ILLMOOR CHRONICLES

The Ratastrophe Catastrophe

DAVID LEE STONE

Hodder
Children's
Books

A division of Hodder Headline Limited

A Catalogue record for this book is available
from the British Library

ISBN 0 340 87397 3

Typeset in NewBaskerville by Avon DataSet Ltd,
Bidford-on-Avon, Warwickshire

Printed and bound in Great Britain by
Clays Ltd, St Ives plc

The paper and board used in this paperback by
Hodder Children's Books are natural recyclable products
made from wood grown in sustainable forests.
The manufacturing processes conform to the
environmental regulations of the country of origin.

Hodder Children's Books
a division of Hodder Headline Limited
338 Euston Road
London NW1 3BH

For my mother,
Barbara Ann Stone.

Selected Dramatis Personae
(ye cast of characters)

Barrowbird	– Distant relative of the forest hornbill.
Burnie	– Troglodyte councillor.
Cadrick, Taciturn	– Trade Minister.
Firebrand, Chas	– Landlord of the Rotting Ferret inn.
Forestall, Tambor	– Council chairman, ex-sorcerer.
Franklin, Victor	– Assassin.
Goldeaxe, Gordo	– Dwarf mercenary.
Green, Mifkindle	– Assassin.
Grim, Bernard	– Rat-catcher.
Marshall, Pegrand	– Manservant to the Duke of Dullitch.
Mick	– Mini-mite.
Modeset, Vandre	– Duke of Dullitch.
Quarrell	– Lord Chancellor of Dullitch.
Quickstint, Jimmy	– Thief/herald. Tambor's grandson.
Phelt, Cedric	– Militia man.
Piddleton, Tommy	– Brat.
Sands, Quaris	– Home Secretary and member of the council.
Siddle, Malcolm	– Rat-catcher's apprentice.
Soak, Rochus the	– Seer.
Stump	– Adventurer.
Teethgrit, Groan	– Barbarian mercenary.
Vicious	– Fox-terrier.
Wustapha, Diek	– Charmer.
Wustapha, Pier	– Farmer, father of Diek Wustapha.
Wustapha, Mrs	– Farmer's wife, mother of Diek.

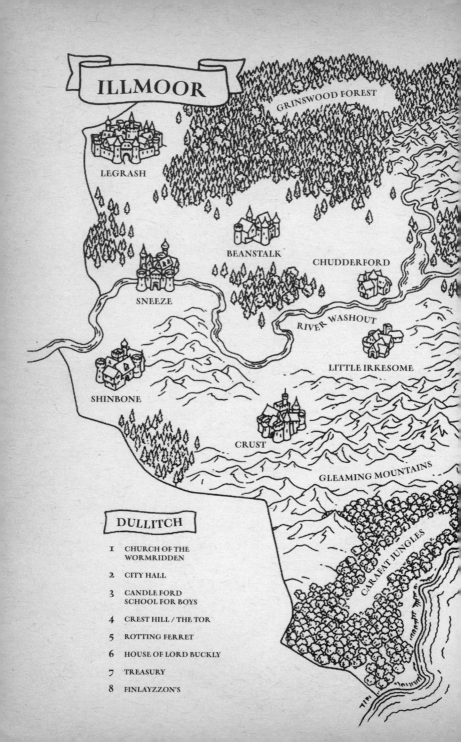

Prologue

During the Tri-age (civilization's third attempt at getting things right) there grew, from the swollen lip of Illmoor, a city quite unlike any other in recorded history.

The rulers of this city were imbecilic, giving rise to crimes as diverse as fraud and murder. Amid this vile assortment of assassins and cutpurses the city quickly earned a grim reputation, becoming spurned by many and generally avoided by travellers throughout the Gleaming Mountains, by which it was sheltered, like the treasure horde of a particularly insecure dragon.

Still, a large, weather-beaten plaque swung back and forth on tired hinges above the city gates proudly welcoming all and sundry to visit Dullitch. Though a

local saying warned, 'You haven't lived until you've visited Dullitch and, after that, you won't want to . . .'

The continent of Illmoor is riddled with magic. Not the empty, inept magic practised by men who believe themselves to be of the ancient (now defunct) order of Sorcery. This is *original, undiluted* magic, on which the continent is constructed.

Two types co-exist: light and dark.

Light magic finds its place in the air, giving rise to galloping unicorns, love charms and fairy groves. It is much sought after by these latter day 'sorcerers' but proves practically impossible to harness, even by those who spend long hours in pursuit of it.

Dark magic, on the other hand, seeks immediately to earth itself in the land it was once used to forge. It is an angry magic, an untamed source, a parasite yearning for a host.

And hosts are rare.

Trees suffice, for their roots go deep, but this is no way for dark magic to travel; it's straightforward, rather boring and nobody gets hurt. No, what dark magic truly requires is susceptible minds. These are a delicacy and, although seldom encountered, are always relished. But dark magic is a reckless lodger; it cares little for the minds it invades.

A particularly powerful charge of dark magic appeared during the reign of Duke Modeset. It arrived almost unnoticed. In fact, only two pairs of eyes in the whole of Illmoor observed its passage.

These belonged to the mercenaries, Groan and Gordo; although their part in the story would not become apparent for some time. Long before *they* had the notion to set their steeds southwards, the magic had found its mind.

A searing wave of energy infiltrated a land of fields and forests, homing in, until . . .

One

. . . whoosh.

Diek Wustapha dropped his flute. The leather-bound book that had been resting on his lap tumbled to the floor and lay open, its pages flapping in the breeze.

'What is it, lad?'

The boy turned and looked up at his father, a lock of curly brown hair covering one eye. His smile was apprehensive.

'I thought I heard something, Dad.'

'That'll be the cattle cart,' said his father.

Mr Wustapha looked out over a broad expanse of west-country farmland, his brow creased. A few cows in the field opposite had wandered over to the gate and were mooching idly about.

'No, it was more like a feeling than a sound. I thought I *felt* something.'

'Well, that'll be your dinner,' his father continued, reflecting on years of terror at the dinner table. Mrs Wustapha was one of a long line of cooks on her mother's side of the family. He hoped fervently she would be the last. 'You know something, boy, when I first met your ma, she used to make puddings the like of which would turn your stomach inside out for days on end.'

'Yes, Dad. So you've told me. Repeatedly.'

'Oh well, fair's fair. You're reading again, I see?'

Diek nodded, sliding his flute under a rock with the heel of his boot. He snatched up the book.

'It's called *Ancient Royal Fables*.'

'Good lad,' said his father, patting the boy affectionately on one shoulder. 'Have you got to the bit where Huud the Wise tells Prince Kelogg to go round up the sheep?'

'No, Dad.'

Diek's father was a great believer in stories, as long as they allowed room for improvization. He found them particularly useful when he wanted his son to do something arduous or unpleasant.

Luckily, there was plenty of source material in the tales of King Huud the Wise. Whatever menial chore Diek found himself faced with, he could guarantee poor Prince Kelogg had been there and done it first.

Diek looked up. His father was waiting patiently, a grin spreading like treacle across his broad face.

'I'll go and round the sheep up now, Dad,' said Diek, with a knowing smile.

He got to his feet and set off towards the north field. His father watched him go.

Diek wasn't a bad lad, he thought, at least, not in the conventional sense. He just dawdled from time to time, lacked direction. Perhaps he *should* take his brother's advice and send Diek to Legrash for the summer, let him experience a bit of the real world. What harm could it do?

He stroked his chin thoughtfully, wondering exactly how much trouble a young boy could get into in a town like Legrash. A boy like Diek. Probably best not to speculate. He whistled a merry tune and headed off to see how his son was getting on with the sheep.

The magic sank into Diek's mind like a stone plunging down a deep well. There it lay low, biding its time with patience born of millennia lingering in empty skies and lurking in dormant hollows.

When, finally, the decision was made to surface, it did so with such reptilian guile that no *human* eye could detect the change. Diek Wustapha, however, was cursed with the ownership of a barrowbird with particularly keen sight.

The barrowbird is a curious creature indeed. One of the High Art's darker throwbacks, it is rumoured to have once been an ordinary scrawny relative of the forest hornbill. Legend holds that on the few occasions throughout history when the gods decided to visit Illmoor, they did so by inhabiting the minds of barrowbirds. On one such occasion, it is said that one particularly spiteful god decided to leave something behind: the curse 'Vocaliss Truthilium', commonly translated as 'I speak as I find'.

And the barrowbird did just that. In fact, it gave a new and terrible meaning to the phrase. No personal comment was beyond it. Despised as a species, these put-downs included such harsh observations as, 'You'll never get a girlfriend unless you actually cut that ear off' and the oft heard, 'If I had a figure like yours, love, I'd stay indoors for the duration'.

Now Diek's own barrowbird was treating him to a baleful stare.

'There's somethin' amiss with your right eyeball,' it chirped. ''S glowin' like an ember, init?'

'Is it?'

Diek blinked and raised a hand to his head. He'd been propped against one corner of the pigpen all morning, watching the truffle hogs misbehaving.

'Maybe I'm coming down with something,' he said, beginning to wander off around the side of the pen. 'I *do* feel a bit odd.'

He reached for his flute and brought the instrument to his lips, but was interrupted before he was able to muster a tune.

'Could be fouleye,' the barrowbird squawked. 'You hear of a lot of folk dyin' from that.'

'*Dying*? It's fatal?'

'Right as mustard. You ask anyone: "How's your daughter, Milly?" "Fouleye took her." "How's your Aunty Ethel?" "Down with fouleye." One minute you can be runnin' around in a field, the next you're a goner. That's usually the females, mind. I never heard of a male taken with it yet.'

'OK, OK. It's probably not that, then.'

Diek produced a single, shrill note from the flute, then stowed it away in his tunic. He didn't feel much like playing today; his heart really wasn't in it.

He sighed and closed his eyes tight, then tentatively opened them again.

'Has it gone?' he asked.

'Has it heck,' said the barrowbird. 'Now they're *both* alight! Cor, stone me. You're not standin' on a lightnin' rod or somethin', are ya?'

Diek took a step back, then looked around.

'I'm not standing on anything,' he said. 'Besides, you noticed it when I was over there.'

The barrowbird put its head on one side.

'Then, if I were you, I'd go and see the apothecary or, come to that, the village witch.'

'A witch? Why would I want to see a witch?'

'Well, first there's the eye thing, and then maybe you could find out why you're such a magnet for the pigs.'

'Huh?'

Turning around on his heels, Diek noticed for the first time that all twelve of his father's hogs had followed him along the length of the pen and were now squatting in a group just beyond the fence. Curious. Usually, they ignored him completely, unless he had scraps.

Diek's visit to the apothecary wasn't entirely successful. The man, like most of the village, largely ignored everything Diek had to say, before supplying him with a strange potion that looked and tasted like curdled milk. He had to take it three times a day, as instructed, or, alternatively, 'whenever he felt a bit odd'.

Diek had always been a loner, but now he took to spending whole days in the fields by himself. He'd given the barrowbird to his father as a birthday present; its insults and depressing forecasts of heinous eye disorders had become unbearably tiresome. Also, it'd started crowing about his increasingly resonant voice and made a pointed comment to the effect that, every time he played a note on the flute, the neighbour's grimalkin came tearing across the Midden Field as though the hounds of hell were after it.

He *had* seen that wretched cat a lot lately.

*

Weeks passed and, as the magic took root inside Diek's mind, it began to surface in a peculiar fashion, giving the boy an almost magnetic personality. Foolish absent-mindedness became thoughtful contemplation, inane and idiotic comments were replaced by clever and insightful witticisms. In short, people began to notice Diek Wustapha.

They would spend a few moments talking with him, then trail after him in large groups, like sheep after a shepherd. This was all much to Diek's astonishment; he'd never had a lot of time for people before. Now they praised him and appreciated his music (not like his father, who only tolerated the odd tune every evening after tea). *These* people wanted more. They would wait quite patiently all day, just on the off-chance of a tune. It wasn't even as if his music was particularly melodic, as Diek would have been the first to admit. On the whole, it tended to comprise a few strangled notes huddling together in mournful misery.

Then, one afternoon, everything changed.

Diek had been playing for Butcha, the baker's niece, when suddenly the music came alive. He didn't even notice it happening; it was simply there at his lips, awaiting release. To the girl's mesmerized delight, he produced tune after tune, melody after melody, song after song. These delicate pieces alighted on the air, twisting and turning in the breeze, carrying for miles over the hills and dales. Slowly, one by one, the villagers of Little Irkesome stopped what they were doing and craned their necks to listen. Then they put down their tools and washboards, snatched up their hats and fastened their walking shoes. The cobbled lanes of the village were suddenly alive with inquiring minds irrevocably drawn to the sound.

By mid afternoon, the entire population of the village stood grouped around an oak tree in the Midden Field, listening to Diek Wustapha weave his tune. And play he did. From that day forth, he knew that nothing in his life would ever be the same again.

So did his parents.

In practically no time at all Diek's talents had become many, from snake-charming to hypnotizing mice. Visitors arrived from a few of the neighbouring villages to watch his skills and hear his music. Deep inside his subconscious the magic was throbbing, turning, gaining momentum. And he carried the flute wherever he went.

He'd taken to playing long, drawn-out melodies too, whimsical at first and then, as the days drifted by, progressively stronger. Melodies were more than just tunes, he discovered; they had an identity all of their own. Melodies were almost magical.

Diek found himself reflecting on things like spiritual reception, the existence of telepathic sheep and, more importantly, his part in the larger scheme of things.

'Everybody's got a place in the big picture, lad,' his

father would say, 'It's just a matter of finding out where you fit in.'

Diek wondered where he *would* fit in, and found himself gazing longingly towards Dullitch, city-capital of Illmoor, with its gleaming spires and megalithic monuments.

Two

It was summer in Dullitch, the air was clean and sobering and the streets were filled with the combined odour of freshly-baked bread and exotic spices. In the Market Place, throngs of hungry patrons queued for the early bargains and a few rogue mongrels gathered for free pastry off-cuts at the baker's serving hatch.

It was the annual Clairvoyants' Awareness Weekend and a fête was being held in tribute of Ouija Mastook, the oldest (and most celebrated) medium on record. The guest of honour was due to arrive at midday and no one knew what to expect. The bandstand was currently being reinforced for an entourage of personal assistants and nursing staff.

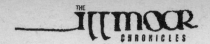

Usually, the ceremony consisted of a rambling speech, three (extraordinarily vocal) cheers and several rounds of celebratory drinks, concluding with a séance in which somebody's Aunt Margaret invariably turned up to let them know that the valuables were hidden in the attic.

Atop the Church of Urgumflux the Wormridden, two members of the dreaded Yowler cult were taking turns to peer through a spyglass at the proceedings below.

The Brotherhood of Yowler was indeed the stuff of nightmares; a ruthless organization rooted in the worship of dark gods who, it was claimed by their shadowy priests, regularly demanded the theft of priceless treasures and a number of ritualistic executions in order to sustain their life-force.

The cultists were, to a man, cloaked assassins, thieves and cutpurses, but their presence in Dullitch was suffered because several of the city's founding families were members. These midnight rogues were extremely well paid and enjoyed considerable support from the council, who turned a blind eye on Yowler-run associations such as Counterfeit House, an academy of condemned forgers, fraudsters and embezzlers, and the Rooftop Runners, a consortium of thieves and murderers.

Mifkindle Green, a junior member of the group, was wasping. This involved dropping in at any large and important gathering, planting a sting (i.e. assassinating the most prominent person) and clearing out quickly to avoid capture. His colleague, Victor Franklin, a known night-runner and poison-dart specialist, was drumming his fingers distractedly on the stonework.

'W-w-will you stop that, Vic?'

'What? Oh, sorry, I just wondered why you hadn't fired yet. You're usually in and out in a cat's sneeze.'

'Shhh. Can't you k-k-keep quiet? You've been really judgemental since you k-k-killed old Banks in that g-graveyard run.'

Mifkindle's gaze returned to the scene, but he wasn't looking down towards the fête. He seemed more interested in the garden of a small cottage on the opposite corner of the street.

'What is it?' Victor persisted, becoming anxious. 'Have we been spotted? Is it the militia? WHAT ARE YOU LOOKING AT?'

'R-r-rats.'

Victor boggled. 'Come again?'

'R-r-ats,' Mifkindle confirmed. 'There's a l-l-line of them heading into the DeLongi place through a g-g-gap in the front wall.'

'Yeah, and?'

'They're w-w-walking in s-single file, like an army. It's odd,' he said, with conviction. 'And I've seen a l-lot of them r-recently. Almost every d-d-day, in fact.'

Victor shrugged. 'Dullitch is a big city,' he said. 'You gotta expect rats.'

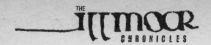

'Not l-l-like th-these.'

Mif kindle passed the spyglass across to his partner, pursed his lips, and waited.

'B-b-big, aren't they?' he said, after a pause.

Candleford School for Boys stood proudly on a slight rise in the north-west corner of the city. It was usually a place of high activity, breaking glass and enthusiastic blasphemy. However, it was the summer holidays and the place was quiet.

In a room crammed with stoves and piled high with crockery, Bernard Grim applied half an ear to the wainscoting and listened intently. His apprentice, a boy called Malcolm, with rugged features and a black eye, watched with mounting trepidation.

'It could be a vole, Mr Grim.'

'Don't be ridiculous, lad. You don't get voles in a workhouse kitchen, who ever heard of such a thing?'

'My uncle had a vole come into his kitchen.'

'Your uncle's no better than he should be.'

'Do you think it could be a rat?' piped up a small, plump maid with golden ringlets and a pork-pie smile.

'Aye,' said Grim, wondering about the unconcealed eagerness in her voice.

'Ain't nothing wrong with my uncle,' said Malcolm sulkily.

Grim ignored him and leaned in closer, raising a finger and tapping tentatively on the woodwork. A scratching began on the other side of the wainscoting.

'He might be eccentric and I know he talks to himself a bit, but he's never done anyone no harm. Well, apart from that Mrs Haveshank and she said she wouldn't be pressin' charges.'

'Quiet, lad! It's on the move; listen.'

The apprentice knelt down beside his employer, face creased with the effort of concentration. Eventually, he gave a reluctant nod.

'Right,' Grim whispered. 'Get me a forty-seven from the cart.'

Malcolm crept out of the kitchen and returned a few moments later, laden with an assortment of wooden planks.

'I couldn't remember which one was which, Mr Grim.'

He passed a plank from the stack to the rat-catcher and waited patiently as Grim balanced it in the palm of his hand.

'That's a sixteen.'

He handed back the plank and rolled his eyes as the apprentice chose another.

'That's a one-seven-four.'

'But they're identical, Mr Grim.'

The rat-catcher turned to the pork-pie maid and offered her a wry smile, but he found no sympathy in those eyes. Despite a moon-like countenance, the woman's face possessed a distinctly odd tinge. She looked absolutely ravenous. Every so often her tongue

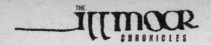

would play over her lips like an affectionate slug. Grim returned his attention to the wainscoting, and found himself hoping the rat had managed to escape.

'Are there cellars below, Miss?'

'There used to be,' the girl said, nodding. 'The principal had them all blocked up when a few of the teachers were caught tutoring after hours.'

Grim tried to focus on the flagging wallpaper. For the first time, he spotted a large yawn in the wainscoting.

'Would you mind leaving us alone now, Miss?' he managed. 'This little experiment shouldn't take long.'

The maid gave a slight nod, lifted her apron and hurried away. The curious smell that Grim had noticed on the way in seemed to depart with her.

'She didn't look too clever, did she?' the rat-catcher whispered conspiratorially. 'I reckon she's been at the stock or something.'

The apprentice looked mystified.

'Why d'you say that?'

'Well, there's a funny smell from her. Didn't you notice it?'

'I did as it happens. I just didn't like to say anything; I thought it might be those scones you had for breakfast.'

The rat-catcher studied the young man's expression for a few moments, then hit him with the one-seven-four. After offering the boy a vicious scowl, he returned his attention to the wainscoting, and froze.

A pair of glowing red eyes were staring back at him; they were attached to the largest rodent Bernard Grim had laid eyes on in more than twenty years in the trade.

'M-m-malcolm,' he managed. 'Forget the wood, get a dagger.'

Afternoon came and went.

'Apprentice to Bernard Grim the rat-catcher, milord.'

The palace guard bowed low and stepped to one side, admitting the scrawny frame of the rat-catcher's assistant. At the opposite end of the long hall, a thin, angular-faced man sat scribbling furiously behind a desk laden with paperwork. He didn't look up when the door closed behind his trembling visitor.

'Sit.'

The command echoed around the hall. Eventually, the man behind the desk stopped scribbling and popped the pen into an inkwell. Then he looked up.

'Not on the *floor*, boy! Get a chair, for heaven's sake.'

The apprentice moved quicker than the eye could see, snatched up one of the chairs and pulled it towards the desk. Then he tucked his cap into a back pocket and sat down, embarrassment playing on his face like sunlight on a pond.

'Now,' said the duke, for this was the title he commanded, 'you wanted to see me about something?'

The boy nodded.

'Well?'

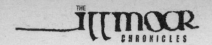

'We caught a rat, milord.'

'Really?' said the duke, proffering the smile he generally reserved for lunatics and tax-evaders. 'And that's unusual, is it?'

Malcolm frowned and reached up to scratch his chin.

'In what way, milord?' he said.

'Well, unless I'm very much mistaken, you are a *rat-catcher*. Surely snaring the odd rodent is all part and parcel of the job, no?'

'Not when they're this size, sir.'

The creature the apprentice proceeded to pull from his trousers was quite unlike anything Modeset had seen before. The duke leaped from his seat and ushered the chair in front of him. He had no desire to suffer the final, frenzied death leap of a half-expired monstrosity.

'Oh, don't worry, milord,' said the boy, reassuringly. 'It's a goner. But there are more of them, we reckon. That's why I've come to see you. They've built a base beneath Candleford School. We heard 'em, this morning. They start goin' at it, they could be all over Dullitch in minutes. I know the council's supposed to deal with this sort of thing and I did try knocking at City Hall, but I don't think anyone's available.'

'Oh?' said Modeset, eyebrows raised.

'There was this wooden board outside the door. It said "Gone Fishing".'

Modeset let out a long sigh. When reflecting on the

council's overall performance of late, 'Gone Fishing' seemed to be an accurate description.

'These, erm . . . these *rats*. There could be an awful lot of them, you say?'

The apprentice nodded.

'Mr Grim, that's my guv'nor, he reckons that if you let it go more than a week you're gonna have to paint whiskers on the Royal Crest.'

'I see. Thank you, young man. That will be all.'

He dismissed the boy, and summoned his servant. After a few moments, a man came hurrying into the room. He was short and stocky with long hair (though none on the top of his head), a well-groomed beard and a fixed, sort of bemused smirk.

'What is it, milord?'

'Pegrand! We have something of a crisis on our hands.'

'Oh gods, no. What is it, the chef?'

Modeset sighed, plucking a copper coin from the table top and employing it to scratch the bridge of his aquiline nose.

'No, Pegrand, not the chef. Don't get me wrong, I *don't* like him and he *has* to go, but this time it's something a little more serious.'

'Okay, milord. I'm all ears.'

'Good. Do you remember those fellows from the Watchtower Patrol, fell in here last week mumbling something about a rat-horde beneath the Poor Quarter?'

'Vaguely, milord.'

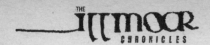
'Have them arrested immediately.'

'Er . . . right, milord. Any particular charge?'

'Oh, I don't know. Causing a disturbance of the peace? Malicious lies? I'm sure you'll think of something.'

'Of course, milord. Is there a problem?'

'Yes, perhaps. There does, in fact, appear to *be* a rat-horde beneath the Poor Quarter, and I don't want any Told-You-Sos stirring up the conspiracy theorists.'

Pegrand Marshall scribbled a note on the pad permanently suspended on a chain attached to his belt.

'Er, won't the act of arresting two watchtower guards stir up the conspiracy theorists, milord?'

'Mmm? What? Well, oh, yes, I suppose it will. What do you suggest?'

'Well, we could rub them out, dump the corpses up past Gate Field and then have two boys from the plough-crew carve out a crop circle round 'em. That way we might have the conspiracy theorists up in arms, but at least they'll have something baseless to talk about.'

'Excellent. Meanwhile, however, we do have a serious problem. This morning's little visit follows three from the merchants, two from the sewer attendants and several from the Yowler Brotherhood. An outbreak of rats is imminent.'

'I'll put the palace on high alert, milord. Anything else I should be doing?'

Modeset nodded gravely.

'Go down to the riverbank and round up the council.

Tell them we have an infestation of giant rats that, despite its humble beginnings, could have designs on the Merchants' Quarter. That should get them suitably anxious. Oh, and let them know time is short; we need a publicly acceptable announcement by Friday evening.'

Modeset took a deep breath, waited for the servant to flitter away, then caressed his eyelids with the rough tips of his fingers. It was obviously going to be one of *those* days.

Morning arrived to find a grim scene at City Hall.

The Dullitch Council stared gloomily at each other over the long debating table. They had been called to the Grey Room at an unspeakable hour and were waiting to shout at anyone who looked even partly responsible.

Eventually the acting chairman, Tambor Forestall, appeared in the doorway. He'd been dreading this ever since his predecessor vacated the premises over a month ago. It was just so typical of his luck. For three years old Gambol had chaired Dullitch Council and, in all that time, not a single catastrophe or even a mild uprising. *He* gets the job and, whizz, a plague of giant rats.

He wasn't being helped by Duke Modeset's latest initiative demanding 'A Council Structure Reflecting the Ethnic Make-up of a Modern Society' either. He cast a worried glance around the room, noting with horror that only four members of the council were human. He recognized a local alchemist, but the barbarian was a total mystery and the cross-species squabbling in the corner he'd already decided to file under 'Politely Ignore'.

A vein throbbed in his temple and his arms were aching, but it was too late to back out now. He banged his gavel hard on the tabletop.

'Gentlefolk,' he began.

'Gadjfjr—'

'We have been called here today—'

'Gktgngn gkkrg jfjf kfg fjy—'

'On a matter of the utmost urgency.'

'Gghf hf h fkf kf frjfjfj.'

Tambor hesitated, driven to distraction by the echo that seemed to accompany his every utterance. Sitting beside him at the table was a warty, green-skinned midget with long, pointed ears and teeth in various stages of decay. His nose looked like a melted candle, and a strange green mucus dripped from the end to the tabletop. It occurred to Tambor that he hadn't seen the creature arrive.

'Excuse me,' he ventured. 'Who *are* you?'

The creature sighed. 'I'm the translator.'

Tambor leaned forward conspiratorially.

'For who?' he said.

'The orc down at the far end,' said the translator. 'He doesn't speak Plain Tongue.'

'What language *does* he speak?'

'Brave. Not that you can call it a language, as such.'

'No Brave for "terrible infestation", then?'

'No,' said the translator. 'Not unless you can squeeze it into words of one syllable.'

Tambor appeared to consider this.

'Fair enough,' he said. 'How about RATS?'

He leaned back and smiled contentedly.

The rest of the council began to sit up and exchange a few concerned glances.

'Right. Everyone listening?' said Tambor forcefully.

'Rats, you say?' shouted a seer, from the far end of the table.

Tambor glared at him. He had a personal dislike of seers for a number of reasons, not least because their largely invented profession had outlived sorcery in Dullitch. Also, they regularly insisted on fanciful names like 'Izmeer of the Swarm' and never seemed to achieve anything that didn't require a lot of skulking about in caverns with a piece of chalk and a far-off look in their eyes.

The seer glared back at him, correctly reading his expression.

'Sounds jolly intriguing,' he said, and turned away to finish his game of cards with the barbarian.

Tambor watched him quietly, then returned his attention to the remainder of the City Council and wished, quite fervently, that he had taken the job at Jimmy Stover's pie shop. Only Quaris Sands, the elderly

Home Secretary, seemed to be paying any attention, though he was mumbling incessantly under his breath, clearly put out by the early call. Tambor groaned.

'All right, everybody,' he said wearily. 'We have a plague of giant rats in Dullitch. It started beneath the Candleford Boys' School, and it's growing at a rate of knots. The Poor District is already in dire straits and the Merchants' Quarter could be next. All the rat-catchers have fled in terror and even the assassins have declined the contract. We're looking to devise some potential solutions to offer to his lordship, the duke.'

The translator raised his hand.

'How about sending in a big cat?' he said.

'I don't actually think you're on the council,' said Tambor. 'Anybody else?'

The translator offered him a scowl, and leaned across to inform the orc representative that Tambor had just insulted its mother.

'It could be an omen from the gods,' said Taciturn Cadrick, the Trade Minister. 'A sign that we should seek spiritual and intellectual fulfilment.'

'So what do we do about it, o wise one?'

'Don't ask me. Perhaps we should try hiring a mercenary to destroy them. How about that barbarian fellow from the Virgin Sacrifice Scandal?'

'No chance,' said the Home Secretary quickly. 'I wouldn't have that lunatic back inside the gates for all the gold in Spittle. It took us months to mop the blood off the clock tower. This city has suffered enough humiliation at the hands of mercen—'

The rest of his sentence was drowned out by screams, which erupted from the almshouses across the street. The council hurried to the windows and looked down at the scene unfolding below. People were pouring out of the small doorway, trampling over each other and screaming for help.

One woman's cry was clearly audible amid the uproar. She was yelling at the top of her voice, 'RATS! RATS! RAAATTSSS!'

As the council looked on, the writhing sea of humanity swarmed towards Market Place, turned a corner and disappeared.

'All right,' said Tambor, massaging an injury he'd picked up during his dash to the window. 'Let's have a vote of hands, shall we? One, two, four, eight – yes, I think we're pretty much decided. I'll get a message to the duke. Perhaps he can decorate things a little, you know, for the public.'

Three

Diek Wustapha was watching three of the village girls watching him. Their names were Trist, Tadrai and Dreena, and they had been following him across hill and dale for the best part of the morning. This was odd, Diek noted, because only weeks before they had thrown a bucket of sheep dip dregs over him and called him names. Now they were trailing mere feet behind him, stopping when he stopped, eyes turning downwards with a curious respect each time he cast a glance over his shoulder. Strange.

Of course, he had been carrying the flute. Although he hadn't actually been *playing* it, he supposed the slightest hint of a note had kept them with him.

He didn't know where this knowledge came from, he simply knew it to be true.

It was the same with sheep; they followed him everywhere. Then again, they were sheep, and sheep will eagerly pursue anyone who looks like they might have a vague idea of where they're headed. But it didn't explain the cows, horses, pigs, dogs, birds, lizards and other, more nondescript, creatures whose fixed attentions he had drawn during the waning week.

Diek came to a sudden stop, cast his gaze back to the group of girls and then down at the instrument resting in his palm.

Play. Won't you play? Won't you, Diek? Play.

The three faces were sullen, lips turned down, and no voice seemed to have risen among them.

Hesitantly, almost reluctantly, he raised the flute to his lips.

'Look at them cows. Now there's a thing.' The barrowbird flapsquawked its way on to Pier Wustapha's shoulder.

Diek's father stood at the door of the cottage and looked out over his broad acres of farmland. Presently, his wife joined him, her face a patchwork of wrinkled confusion.

'What're they doing, love?' she managed, aghast.

The question produced a shrug from her husband and a thoughtful scowl from the barrowbird.

'Beats me, love,' said Pier. 'It looks like they're making for the field nearest Olvi's Place.'

'Why would they do that, d'you think?'

Pier Wustapha shook his curly head.

'I've no idea. There's nothing much over that way, apart from—'

His wife waited for an end to the sentence, but none came.

'Apart from what?' she prompted.

Pier scratched at his bottom lip with a jagged fingernail.

'Well,' he said, uncertainly, 'I saw young Diek go off that way this very mornin'. They could be followin' after him like Mibbit's dog and the cat as hangs around the farm. Seems like every livin' thing's taken after the lad. Even old Tyler's daughters were on the trot when I last spied 'em.'

'Oh no.' Mrs Wustapha rolled her eyes. 'Not them again! What *is it* with the lad?'

Pier lanced a boil with an overgrown fingernail.

'He's his father's son and no mistake,' he said.

Mrs Wustapha frowned. She didn't look so sure.

'Play some more, Diek, won't you play some more?'

The words had definitely come from Dreena this time. She and her siblings had Diek surrounded, his back hard against the gnarled bole of an oak tree. The flute was clasped firmly in his fist, but Dreena had closed a hand over his wrist. Her other hand was at his mouth, delicate fingers tracing the line of his lips.

'Won't you play for us, Diek? Won't you?'

Her pool-blue eyes were piercing his soul; he felt like a rabbit caught in the trapper's mechanical jaw, awaiting the inevitable. And all the while, a voice, *the* voice, seared through his thoughts like a hot blade: *you can have anything, Diek Wustapha, anything you want. All you have to do is . . .*

'Diek!'

His father's voice, distant but determined.

All you have to do . . .

'Diek, lad!'

Closer now, a lot closer.

All . . .

'Diek!'

A sharp slap burned his cheek, and Diek awoke from his reverie. The girls had drifted away to make room for his father, who was shaking him as if fearful that he might have descended into a swoon.

'That's it, lad,' his father was saying. 'That's it, you hear me? It's time you went away from here, got yourself a place in the world. There's something badly amiss with you, boy, and I'm damned if your mother an' I are gonna get thrown out o' the village because of it.'

Four

Duke Modeset, reluctant ruler of Dullitch and its bubonic environs, reclined in his marble throne and gazed absent-mindedly at the large family crest over the fireplace; a regular splash of rainwater appeared beneath it during every shower. It was a sign of the times. Recently, the payment of city taxes had become so rare that the palace staff had been forced to plug leaks with such finery; the once grand fireplace had been an early casualty in the war against bad weather.

Far off to the east, an explosion of unnecessarily dramatic proportions signalled the arrival of more daily experiments from the Bridleway Gunpowder Factory. The duke smiled inwardly and jumped up with renewed vigour to face the onslaught of another soggy Dullitch morning.

He squinted, coughed and yelled for the post. Then, remembering the servants' favoured delay in responding to commands, went to fetch it himself. The contents of the royal letter box turned out to be three tax demands addressed to a certain Herbert Nofesit, a notice of enrolment from the Church of Urgumflux the Wormridden, and a letter from Tambor Forestall, council chairman, notifying him of the city's official line on the rat situation.

Modeset's hawkish features fell foul of a frown; it was very unusual for the council to put anything in writing, let alone provide multiple-choice solutions and several small boxes requiring the royal seal. Their new chairman must be quite the ticket. Slowly, however, the duke's smile returned. It appeared that the council leader had mistakenly dispatched the original draft of his letter which, bereft of secretarial correction, read:

Dear Lord Madshat,

The council and I are fully aware that you are by way of being a little mentally challenged, so we'll avoid using long sentences in order to make this letter very simple . . .

City = Problem = PLAGUE OF RATS.

SOLUTION	POSSIBLE/KNOWN DRAWBACKS
1) Hire a rat-catcher	*There is not a rat-catcher in the entire city who'll go near a job like this with a ten-foot barge pole.*
2) Send in the militia	*Of our 1,004 militiamen, 1000 are currently deployed in the Mountains of Mavokhan in our war against Phlegm, and the other four are off sick.*
3) Burn affected areas	*This is not really a solution in itself, as burning down all affected areas of the city would leave just the palace and Joe Donn's Bakery.*
4) Hire Mercenaries	*None. Mercenaries do just about anything for the right price, and several of the household names are known to be at large in the hills around Dullitch at this time.*

Best wishes,
Tambor Forestall, Chair.

Modeset finished reading the letter, sighed and rang for his manservant. Pegrand Marshall arrived presently, a silver platter in one hand and, for reasons probably best left unknown, a plunger in the other.

'You pulled, milord?'

Modeset was shaken from his reverie. 'Mmm? Oh, no, Pegrand. Not in a long, long time.'

The manservant showed a marked interest in the carpet.

'No, the bell, sir. You pulled the *bell*.'

'Ahh yes, so I did. Get my carriage, will you? We need to pay a long overdue visit to City Hall; it appears the council have drawn up a selection of passable actions for our rat crisis and they require my seal.'

'I see, milord. Does that actually demand a personal appearance?'

'Mmm? No, it does not. However, I have chosen the option of hiring mercenaries and I would like to ensure that our good friends in the council recruit the, how can I put it, correct breed of scumbag for the job. Does that sound right?'

'Absolutely, milord. After the Virgin Sacrifice Scandal—'

'Exactly.'

'What was his name again?'

'Umm, Teethgrit, I believe; a suitably heinous name. Shall we go?'

Deep beneath Dullitch, the rodent tide began to swell, driven on by the urgency to feed. They tumbled over one another in their haste to reach the surface, forming a terrible frenzied carpet that flowed inexorably upwards.

Five

The Dullitch North Gate was haemorrhaging heralds. They rode forth in every direction, each one privately more determined than the others to return with the city's saviour; each one secretly wondering just how much they could decrease the reward money, in order to snag a small accumulation of personal wealth.

The most successful of these was a gangly, greasy youth named Jimmy Quickstint. He rode the fastest, youngest and most agile of the horses, though, because of his natural inferiority complex, *he* thought it the cripple of the bunch. Jimmy had, in an illustrious career spanning more than three years, worked as a window-cleaner, a baker's assistant, an apprentice alchemist and journeyman to an insane toy maker with designs on world domination. He currently spent his nights engaged in an eager bid for membership of Yowler's elite thievery consortium and his days serving burnt fry-ups at Spew's Breakfast Bar. Occasionally (on a Wednesday afternoon as a rule), he also found time to be the most despised of the city heralds. He didn't know very much about horses, which goes a little way to explain why he had no clue that he was a good mile ahead of his nearest rivals. He had even less of a clue that two of Illmoor's most infamous mercenaries were leaving a village along his current path and he would soon be accosted by them. Some knowledge you can do without.

The road out of Spittle was notorious. It wound its way along the floor of a wide valley surrounded by lush and verdant woodland. Here and there ancient standing stones would mark rises in the road, an idea employed by Duke Modeset's elderly predecessor. Despite the fragrant air and sweet serenity of the surroundings, no one except the poor or the suicidal ever travelled this way; the road was a breeding-ground for bandits.

Gordo Goldeaxe put his head on one side and squinted. A poster was nailed to one of the trees, fluttering in the breeze. He reached up and ripped it down.

'Wanted For Crimes Against Alchemy,' he said, reading aloud. 'Leaven Grismal. Reward if believable explanation given to Society of Alchemists.'

Footsteps approached, and a sword was embedded in a patch of ground beside the tree, up to the hilt. A palm the size of a melon gripped the dwarf's shoulders and lifted a stout battleaxe off its half-rotted strap, where it had been hanging precariously for the last half an hour, causing Gordo's companion no end of annoyance.

'Thanks,' said the dwarf.

A nod.

'Looks like your typical idiot gold-brewer,' Gordo continued, attempting to read the small print on the poster with little success. 'Don't suppose there's much money in it.'

His companion said nothing.

'Is there something wrong with you, Groan?'

The dwarf looked up at a man of immense proportions. Muscles jostled for position in every limb, like snakes trying to escape from a sack. The overall impression was marred, however, by a crocheted bobble hat that perched atop the warrior's head like a cherry on a cup cake.

'You've been miserable all week,' said Gordo, removing his helmet and tucking it under one arm. 'Ever since you saw that magic rainbow thingy just past Irkesome.'

'Yeah well, you know 'ow it is. I don't trust magic,

'specially when it comes from the clouds. 'S bad enough when we 'ad sorcerers firin' off spells left right an' centre, now we've got all the raw stuff back. Can you 'magine what'd 'appen if that blast 'ad've hit us?'

'Well it didn't. It hit some stranger down in the valley.'

Groan frowned.

'How'd you know?'

'I saw it through the telescope. I didn't show you because you were waving that sword around like a lunatic. Oh, and speaking of lunacy, where exactly did you get that hat?'

'Killed an orc up by the Scoon,' said Groan, flossing his teeth with a length of happas. The warrior awarded great attention to his teeth and, indeed, those belonging to other people. 'This was all he had on him.'

The dwarf appeared to consider this.

'Couldn't you have just left it there?'

There was something odd about the way the warrior just shrugged off the observation. Gordo was undeterred. When it came to taking hints, the dwarf wasn't the quickest of companions. The only drifts caught by his family were the kind you had to remove with a shovel.

Groan stared down at him long and hard. Then he removed the hat. The hills echoed with laughter.

'How did that happen?' said Gordo, when he'd managed to regain control of himself.

'You remember that dragon up at Vale Wake?'

'You said it missed you.'

'I lied.'

There were approximately ten hairs left on Groan Teethgrit's once lock-laden scalp. He looked crestfallen.

'Cheer up,' said Gordo, patting the warrior companionably on the kneecap and staring up at his vacant expression. 'It could be worse.'

Somehow, the statement lacked conviction.

'Horse up ahead,' said Gordo, changing the subject. 'Maybe more than one. You know what that means?'

Groan frowned.

'Yeah,' he said. 'It means we'll have somethin' to ride to the next village.'

A sudden flash of inspiration brought the dwarf to a standstill.

'Why don't we just go back to Spittle and take that air balloon the locals were mucking about with?' he said. 'There's no reason to kill anyone, we could just storm the square and . . . what?'

Groan raised one eyebrow, a particularly expressive gesture for a man whose discourse was usually limited to a succession of grunts. He shrugged.

'What I mean is,' Gordo continued, 'that we can't attack on the road. Remember? The only folk who use the road these days are thieves and the local militia, and we can't afford any more trouble with Dullitch, not after that mess-up with the Virgin Sacrifices. I still have nightmares about *that*. Whereas, if we get the balloon . . .'

'I ain't gettin' no b'loon. B'loons is for stubbin' clowns an' I look enough of a dillo in this hat.'

'Oh, come on, buddy. At least think about it.'

Groan gave the situation a moment's thought. It was over in seconds.

'We'll attack the riders,' he said. 'That's what they're there for.'

'I vote we don't attack,' said Gordo.

Groan shook his head.

'I wanna fight,' he said. 'An' kill folk.'

'Right, fair play. So that's one vote for you and one for me, giving me the majority.'

Gordo noticed his companion's confused expression.

'Remember how I told you to work it out?' he said.

The horse was slowing; having been present at a number of notable land wars, it had an instinct for trouble. However, Jimmy Quickstint didn't know this, so he dug in his heels and tried to urge it onwards.

Suddenly, there was an obstruction in the road. At first Jimmy took it for a mountain troll, but then he noticed the crocheted bobble hat and the leopard-skin posing pouch. Another distinguishing oddity, on closer inspection, appeared to be a barracuda tooth on a nipple ring.

'First, get off the 'orse, or die,' it said. 'Then you can

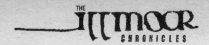

'and over all yer gold, or die. You'll 'ave noticed that two of them . . . er . . . six options is you dyin'. Make yer choice.'

Jimmy brought the horse to a stop (at least, he meddled with the reins a little; the horse had actually stopped moving a few minutes before).

'What do you want?' he said, feeling rather stupid and fearing another options-based summary of the situation.

Groan looked momentarily taken aback. He wasn't used to having to repeat himself.

'Hang on, I know you!' Jimmy continued, his voice edged with genuine glee. 'You're Groan Teethgrit, the barbarian who got thrown from the Crest Tower after that business with the virgins!' The thief slapped his thigh, gave a little whistle and grinned like a hyena. 'What happened to that fat, one-eyed dwarf you used to hang out with? What was his name? Cordy?'

'Gordo,' said Gordo, emerging from the undergrowth beside the path. His planned ambush had been rudely interrupted by the thief's 'fat, one-eyed dwarf' description. 'And I'd thank you to keep personal remarks to a minimum while I'm carrying this battleaxe, you'll find it protects against accidental decapitation.'

Jimmy held out his hands in a conciliatory gesture.

'I don't want any trouble,' he said, the corners of his mouth turning nervously upward. 'In fact, I've been looking for you two. That is, looking indirectly. I bring a message from Duke Modeset and the Dullitch Council.'

'I'm not deliverin' no message,' Groan snapped. 'Do I look like one of them harolds?'

Gordo tugged at his partner's elbow.

'No, I think he means that *he*'s got a message for *us*. Is that right?'

'Sort of,' Jimmy managed. 'It's a message for several local mercenaries. Dullitch has been infested by a plague of giant rats. We need someone to go into the sewers and wipe them all out.'

'What's the pay like?' Gordo asked, almost before Jimmy had finished speaking.

The thief considered lying about the reward money, but quickly thought better of it. Instead, he whipped a scroll from his saddlebag and unfurled it.

'Says here twenty gold crowns,' he began.

'Twenty? But that's absolutely—'

'Per rat.'

There was a momentary silence.

'Plus a thousand crowns reward money for disposing of the entire horde.'

There followed an even longer pause.

'This mercenary list . . . how, um, how many names have you got on it?' said Gordo, speaking slowly and carefully.

Jimmy performed a quick finger-count.

'Seven,' he said eventually. 'You, your friend, Sven Sussussafson—'

'Dead,' Groan interrupted. 'Taken out by a dragon on the Loft Rise.'

'OK.' The thief nodded. 'I'll cross that one off. Er . . . Ffaff Qumray?'

Gordo shook his head. 'Mutilated by a skeleton horde up near Skoquement; terrible thing for a man to go through, 'n' all. They actually sawed his leg off usin' his other leg.'

'I see. Well . . . then we've got Porridge Riley.'

'Orcs, I'm afraid. Absolute barbarism; they only ever found an ear.'

'Stabb the Brave?'

'Over a cliff in Chudderford.'

'Cordwyn Styke?'

'Wife did him.'

Jimmy sighed deeply and gave a dismissive shrug.

'Well, that just leaves you boys,' he muttered, looking up from the scroll. 'Will you come?'

Groan and Gordo glanced at one another.

'We might be able to fit it in,' said the dwarf.

Jimmy made to snatch up the reins, then hesitated.

'There's only one problem,' he said.

'Yeah, what's that?' said Groan, always ready for a confrontation. The hair he didn't have bristled.

'Well, there's only this one horse, and it can't really take all three of us.'

'That's not a problem,' Gordo shrugged. 'You can walk back.'

Six

Meanwhile, the rumours of Dullitch's swelling rodent infestation began to spread. They started innocently enough, as all rumours do. Bernard Grim was quick to swear his hapless (nay *hopeless*) apprentice to secrecy but, as fate would have it, Malcolm talked in his sleep.

He also shared rooms with Thomas Dimchurch, above the baker's shop in Furly Lane.

Thomas, a member of the notorious Rooftop Runners, was the very soul of discretion. His strictly employed code of secrecy meant that he kept a vouch safe to the grave. However, he *had* recently tripped on Malcolm's discarded sandal and broken his leg, incapacitating him and forcing him to withdraw from a

date with Trissa Lefyette at Gamerade, Dullitch's premier restaurant. So, in a moment of anger and frustration, he repeated the apprentice's mutterings in a hushed whisper to Chas Firebrand, the owner of the Rotting Ferret tavern. In all probability, *that* was the turning point.

Chas had a mouth; it wasn't a *big* mouth but it was a mouth with ambitions. Anything you told Chas could be relied upon to stay between you, himself and just about anyone else the man laid eyes on.

Within a few days, word had spread from Dullitch and its swarming environs, across Illmoor, as far as Legrash.

Dullitch is under attack. Dullitch is under siege. Dullitch is infested with . . .

'Rats?' Diek Wustapha raised one chiselled eyebrow in mock amusement. He'd left his home for the neighbouring town of Crust with his parents' blessing, a week's worth of bread and cheese and enough gold at least to afford him shelter. 'But rats are relatively harmless, aren't they?'

The villager with the foul breath he'd been talking to boggled at him.

'What? Haven't you ever 'eard of the Great Fire of Dullitch?'

Diek nodded. 'Of course.'

'Well, it was rats what pulled that off. Well-known fact.'

'Hmm . . . I thought a baker started it.'

'Yeah, but some folk reckon he was a rat by day.'

Diek thought about this and decided not to pursue the matter. The fact was that there appeared to be strong rumours of a hostile infestation in Dullitch, and there was also a sizeable treasury. You didn't need to be a mathematician to count the odds. 'And people are frightened, you say?'

'Oh yes, *terrified*,' the villager continued. 'Word is, they're afraid to walk the streets and they're too scared to stay inside because the rats are coming through the floorboards. That's mainly them who's poor an' lives by the downstream. O'course, uptown all the rich're plannin' a big ol' protest on account o' findin' out what the duke an' the council are gonna do 'bout it all.'

'I see. How do you know all of this, exactly?'

The villager offered another shrug and pointed east towards the town hall.

'Heralds,' he said simply. 'Two arrived from the city this morning. O'course, I'd already 'eard most of it on the grapevine by then.'

Diek looked around him. He'd planned to stay a little longer in the village but now, on reflection, there didn't seem to be any point. Dullitch beckoned, and Diek felt compelled to entrust himself to fate . . . and the voice which called him, ever so gently, to task.

He thanked the villager for his help, and made his way over to the town hall.

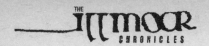
Evidently, Dullitch's infestation hadn't drawn that many eager saviours. In fact, of the five men queuing to sign up for mercenary duties in the Crust Town Hall, only Diek had all his limbs. Still, it seemed that a lifetime passed before the other hirelings staggered, hopped and (in one case) *clawed* their way away from the table.

Diek swallowed, tightened his grip on the flute, and stepped up to the seated herald.

'Name?'

'Diek Wustapha.'

He tried hard not to watch the herald's bushy eyebrows mating as he scribbled Diek's name down with a quill.

'Division?'

'Um, I don't quite understand.'

The herald leaned back in his chair and folded both arms.

'If you're a mercenary, you have to fit into some sort of category.'

'Such as?'

'Well, such as Assassin, Warrior, Barbarian, Mercenary, Exterminator, Vermin Expert? What?'

'I'm none of those things!'

The herald was beginning to look mildly annoyed.

'Then how do you propose to rid our city of rats?'

'Using this.' Diek proffered the flute and tried to look confident.

'What is it?'

'My flute. I play, people follow.'

'Just people?'

'Animals too. Donkeys, horses, rabbits. Maybe even—'

'Rats?'

'Yes. I hope so.'

The herald nodded.

'Then you're a Charmer,' he said. 'Sounds good; it's certainly worth a try. You're the only Charmer, so far. You can come back to Dullitch with me. I'll send a cart for the rest of the sign-ups, not that it's worth it.'

He rolled up the scrap of parchment he'd been writing on and motioned over to the mercenary who'd clawed away just before Diek had stepped up. He was still only halfway to the door.

The heralds weren't messing about. They'd been given specific instructions and a non-negotiable timeframe in which to achieve them. Within a few minutes of signing up to the cause, Diek found himself thundering towards the distant spires of Dullitch on a horse that, although grand, seemed oblivious to any obstacle until they'd actually hit it. When the herald eventually indicated a resting point in the middle of Bunkly Wood, Diek had to spend three-quarters of an hour plucking thistles and snapped-off branch ends from his neck and chest. The horse seemed fine.

Duke Modeset was staring down his nose, a habit that tended to develop after any length of time spent

conversing with members of the Dullitch Council. Having dropped in at the City Hall and found them all out 'on civic duties', he'd eventually had to dispatch a handful of road-wardens with the task of retrieving at least one official and bringing him, her or *it* to the palace. They'd located Tambor Forestall in double quick time, dragging him (kicking and screaming by all accounts) from the gambling room of a local inn.

'So you sent word . . .' the duke began, '*before* you actually had my approval?'

'Erm . . . yes, milord. I thought it would look bad for you if we dallied about, you know how it is with politics.'

'Hmm . . . interesting. You've seen to things personally, I trust?'

'Oh yes. Absolutely!' said Tambor. 'Heralds have been sent in all directions. Not merely in an attempt to recruit existing mercenaries, but also to scout for any other relevant . . . talentists?'

'There's no such word in the language.'

'No, milord, but I'm sure you see what I mean.'

Modeset sneered at an open ledger on his desk. He was in two minds whether to offer the man a drink (Forestall was edging dangerously close to the decanters), but decided against it on grounds of rumour. It was speculated that Tambor enjoyed his drink, often at the expense of a good suit.

'So,' he said. 'I take it we'll hear from these heralds tomorrow.'

'Heard from them yesterday,' Tambor blurted, obviously regretting the statement as soon as it escaped from his lips.

'Excellent!' said Modeset, visibly shocked. 'Any encouraging responses thus far?'

'Well, we've had three,' said the chairman, producing a scrap of parchment and leaning over the desk to pass it across, 'and we're still waiting on some of the slower carrier pigeons; a few of the newer heralds aren't that sure how to use them. All from outsiders, naturally.'

'Hmm . . . yes, so I see.' Modeset squinted at the parchment, looked over at Tambor, and continued. 'The usual gaggle of knights from Bree, asking for half the kingdom and their expenses paid, a couple of mercenaries, and a young foreigner with a name I wouldn't even try to pronounce . . .'

'We think you say it "Dick", chancellor,' said the chairman, helpfully.

'I see. There doesn't seem to be a title next to his name.'

Tambor scratched his beard thoughtfully. 'To tell you the truth,' he said, concealing the urge to grimace. 'We don't reckon much on that particular applicant.'

'Why not?'

'He's just a young chap from the countryside, reckons he can charm folk by blowing on his flute.'

'In public?' Modeset said, aghast. 'Surely there's some sort of law . . .'

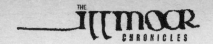
Tambor shook his head. 'Strange folk, countrysiders,' he muttered, as a few shards of daylight infiltrated the arched windows of the palace. 'If you ask me, milord, they're all a bit haystacks.'

'This report; it says here that these people actually follow him around. How extraordinarily eccentric.'

Tambor gave a nod of agreement 'Quite a sight too, I imagine.'

'Absolutely disgusting,' said the duke.

'It's not just the villagers, either,' said Tambor. 'Sheep, pigs, cattle, dogs, rabbits; they all trail after him apparently.'

'Could be he's a personality magnet,' said Modeset.

Tambor scowled. 'Well if he *is*, it certainly hasn't affected the heralds,' he said. 'The one who sent this message thinks he's a bit of a weirdo.'

The two officials shared a moment of silence, as Tambor rummaged through the fathomless depths of his robe in search of a pipe.

'I'm assuming you don't want us to try a few more ordinary measures first?' he said eventually.

Modeset smiled humourlessly.

'What's the point?' he said. 'We don't want to send in rat-catchers or assassins only to have them return with bubonic plague. Also, rather unhelpfully, our twitchy friends over in Legrash have refused all trade with us until some sort of resolve is assured.'

'That bad, is it?'

'It would seem so, yes. This proposed mercenary band is to be paid suicide rates for the disposal of the plague. Their coffer allocation is to be considered bottomless.'

Tambor raised his eyebrows as a crash erupted from deep within the palace. A glass ornament toppled over the duke's grand mantelpiece and shattered. Evidently dinner was being served, or else the rats had reached the palace. Either way, it was time to leave.

It was late afternoon in Dullitch and the crowds were beginning to ebb away. This was due in no small part to the two mercenaries striding down Palace Street. An air of impending doom surrounded them, but that wasn't unusual in Dullitch; anyone who *didn't* have that air was quickly arrested and executed: occasionally the other way around.

'Look at this! They're everywhere.'

Groan and Gordo were kicking rats out of the way with every second step. They had been told to head for the palace, where they would be 'received with true Dullitch Hospitality'. Gordo hoped that this wouldn't be the case (he knew that 'Dullitch Hospitality' generally involved a three-hour wait in a dingy cell before some antique gaoler arrived to spit a pardon all over them).

'I was thinking about that fight we had in Phlegm,' he said to Groan, trying to take his mind off the palace. 'I reckon we'd have won that and no mistake.'

'Reckon you're right,' said Groan, forehead creased as the Basic Vocabulary Fairy attempted to battle redundancy. Groan had been in good spirits since he'd stolen a helmet from a quivering youth on guard at the Market Gate. He offered Gordo a gaping grin.

'Half an apple?' said a voice behind them.

'Anyway,' Groan continued, ignoring the interruption. 'I don't reckon that baron was up to much. We'd 'ave 'ad to kill 'im.'

'Granted. There's plenty of those border lords that owe us a few bob. Take the fat Earl from down Shade Way, we was more than fair with him, considering.'

Gordo looked up at his companion.

'You still got his head?' he asked.

Groan massaged his jaw and shrugged.

'Dunno.'

'Half an apple?' said a voice, persistently.

The two companions parted to admit a slight, dirty-looking rogue wearing a rapidly expiring tunic and grinning like a stowaway cat on a fishing trawler. He gave them a two-fingered salute.

'Half an apple?' he said once more.

'No fanks,' said Groan.

The stranger frowned.

'I'm not offering,' he said. 'I'm asking. I'm a beggar. Have you got half an apple I could borrow?'

'Why half?' said Gordo, intrigued.

'Well, I didn't want to ask for too much.'

'Why borra?' said Groan, who could frown for his country.

'Well, when I said *borrow*,' the beggar continued, 'I was speaking figuratively, like.'

'So you want half an apple to *keep*?' asked Gordo, suspiciously.

'Yep, if it's not too much trouble. Now that you mention it, I could let you have it back in a few days, but I don't suppose you'd like it.'

'What would you do with the uvver arf?' said Groan, still loitering at the beginning of the conversation.

'He wouldn't have two halves, would he?' Gordo reasoned. 'He'd only have half the one we gave him.'

The beggar looked wretched.

'Well?' he said eventually.

'Well what?'

'Can I have half an apple or not?'

'We haven't got one!' Gordo snapped.

The beggar was silent for a moment. Then he offered them an alternative two-fingered salute and disappeared down a side alley.

Groan and Gordo arrived at a corner where a few of the outlying market stalls were packing away for the evening. The dwarf looked back over his shoulder and scowled as three cloaked figures shrank back into the shadows. He'd always had a distinct loathing for Dullitch, and this visit was proving no exception.

Seven

Dullitch was seething with rats.

There were rats on the street, rats running along the window ledges, rats in the gutters. Diek couldn't believe his eyes: the legendary city capital had fallen to an enemy the size of a gnome's boot. No one could have predicted it.

You can remove them. Diek hadn't heard the voice since he'd left Little Irkesome. Now it spoke in a reduced, raspy tone; it was almost snake-like.

The herald reined in his horse and reached out for the reins of Diek's own beast of burden.

'You can get off here 'n' make your own way to the palace. I'll need to check the horses back in.'

Diek found himself practically shoved off his mount; he had to jump two rats and dodge a frying pan aimed from a first-floor window at a third, before he managed to catch up with the herald.

'Aren't you going to take me to the palace?' he asked.

'Nope. Duke's granted an audience to all mercenaries at five o'clock sharp. Don't be late.'

'But I don't know my way around!'

'Your way around what?'

'The city!'

The herald boggled at him.

'There *is* no way around the city, lad. Dullitch is a absolute maze; just find a tavern and wait 'til five, then head for the palace. It's the big spiky thing in the distance.'

Diek watched in a silent and bewildered rage as the herald urged the horses down the street. Then he looked around for a tavern. There didn't seem to be a great shortage of those; in fact, Diek could only see one building on the street that *didn't* look like a tavern, and that turned out to be a brothel. He wandered up and down outside the less rowdy bars (the ones that didn't keep vomiting corpses on to the cobbles) and eventually headed for a single, solitary door that sported a small wooden board proclaiming:

The Rotting Ferret
Est. 824/Prop: Mr C. Firebrand

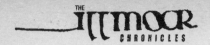

Bring your own stool.
Please make every effort to mop up any of your own blood.
Be careful as you go down; steps are very steep (giants are
advised to watch their heads, dwarfs their arses).
This bar does not encourage fighting, but actively
supports it.
NOTHING TO SEE HERE.

Diek sighed; unfortunately, it was the best of a bad
bunch. He turned the handle and made to go in. As he
did so, he felt a surge of sudden confidence. The voice
was ringing in his ears. *Onward*, it urged. *Down into the
bar. They will cower before us.*

Groan Teethgrit and Gordo Goldeaxe had a lifetime's
experience of violent taverns and, if asked to pick the
most acutely *evil* drinking pit in the entire expanse of
Illmoor, they would undoubtedly have settled on the
Rotting Ferret. Death wasn't just a regular occurrence
there; the business enjoyed a twenty per cent discount at
Domino's Funeral Parlour (located, rather conveniently,
in an alley that paralleled the street on which Ferret
customers tended to land face first).

The place was a dive, an underground drinking pit
which gave shelter to thieves, assassins and a variety of
other miscreants. It also boasted the largest mixed
species clientele in Dullitch; there were elves, ogres,
trolls, orcs, goblins, sprites, pixies and woodlings.

Occasionally, you even got the odd tooth fairy (though they seldom stayed until closing time).

Groan was having a very good day; first he'd seen an attractive barmaid balancing two large jugs on her chest and then he'd been delighted to see Grid Thungus, a rangy barbarian who'd worked for the same warlord over in Legrash. Neither of them had been paid so, in barbarian terms, they had a great deal to talk about. The conversation went something like this:

'Groan, wass happenin'?'

'Nuffin'. You get paid fer that Legrash job?'

'Nah.'

'Me neither.'

'See you 'round.'

'P'raps.'

Gordo was annoyed; he couldn't get a word in edgeways. Instead, he decided to forge a path to the bar. He was halfway through the crowd when a voice rang out over the fray and the entire room fell silent.

Every now and then, on evenings filled with dreadful song and riotous carnage, Chas Firebrand would ask himself why, why, *why* he had elected to own an alehouse in Dullitch. On these occasions, he remembered the time a vile goblin horde had celebrated Sasnack by slitting each other up, or the time when Goff and the Capland Orcs had cajoled Mauler the troll into a game of cat-and-mouse with Wild Sue. It worked both ways, of

course. Some nights he'd freely admit that bartending was the only life for him. But this was mid afternoon, a time when you could usually expect a bare minimum of trouble. Well, not today, evidently, because the young man who had just strode into the bar was either irretrievably stupid or homicidally insane . . .

Eight

You could have heard a pin drop. Every eye in the house was fixed on the young stranger standing in the centre of the room. He stood tall (for his height) and proud, but remained a veritable portrait of vulnerability. Chas Firebrand leaned forward and put one beer-stained hand to his ear.

'Could you repeat that, son?' he said.

'Certainly, humble bartender. I wish for one of the lesser classes seated in this establishment to announce me at the palace. It won't take very long and for the privilege I will spare his life.'

On any other day this speech would have been suicide, plain and simple. A knife in the back if Diek was lucky,

a knife somewhere else if he wasn't. Today was worse. Out of the corner of his eye, Chas noticed that the local thug ring were assembling for a late lunch and, at a corner table, he spotted several likely-looking Yowlers. Chas twitched nervously; it was only a matter of time.

Two shapes loomed into view behind the foreigner, one unquestionably dwarfish and the other implausibly muscular.

Diek smiled confidently as a number of drawn daggers disappeared into pockets and sleeves.

' 'Scuse us,' said Gordo, shoving his way past. He looked up at Diek Wustapha. 'I think this, er, master assassin'll want us to announce him at the palace. Yes?'

The bar, as one, looked momentarily doubtful.

'Um, yes,' Diek said, voice beginning to waver. 'You will be adequate, possibly.'

'I'd get over to a table pretty sharpish if I were you, lad,' Gordo whispered. 'Cos talkin' like that in a place like this is gonna get you nailed up real, real quick.'

Diek's expression changed to one of confusion. His confidence seemed to desert him and, eyes glazed, he began to sidle towards the nearest vacant table. A number of undesirables made to pursue him, but Groan put a hand to his sword hilt and they quickly reconsidered. Diek reached the table and slumped down on to a stool. Slowly, the noise filtered back into the bar.

Groan sighed, sniffed and shoved his way to the bar, Gordo shuffling along in his wake. Most of the conversations had resumed, aside from one being undertaken by a group of zombies in a darkened corner, but this was nothing unusual. One of their number had muttered a few syllables just after lunch and was unlikely to complete the sentence by closing time.

'Toofache, please,' Groan said, arriving at the bar.

Gordo climbed up on to a stool and gave Chas a sympathetic grin.

'It's an old barbarian joke,' he said. 'Don't for juggers' sake get it wrong.'

Chas mumbled under his breath and smiled back.

'What'll it be, gents?'

'Two, er no, better make that three, ales,' said Gordo. 'That kid's going to need a drink.' He rested his battleaxe on the top of a nearby stool. 'Groan, you better go and see if he's all right. He *is* a foreigner, after all. There might be some money in it.'

As the barbarian lurched off in the direction of the table, Gordo turned back to the barman.

'How do we get in to see the duke ahead of any competition?' he said.

Chas pointed over towards a table where a figure sat slumped over a mug half filled with ale, the other half having plastered his beard to the table.

'See that bloke over there? He usually sobers up by five; he might go straight to the palace when he leaves.'

'Why, who is he?' asked Gordo, stepping aside as

Groan returned, supporting the foreigner with a ham-sized grip on his shoulder.

'That's Tambor Forestall, Chairman of the City Council.'

Groan raised what was left of an eyebrow.

'And he drinks in 'ere?'

'Yes.'

Gordo frowned. 'Doesn't he get a lot of attention for being in charge of the council?'

'Nope.'

'Why not?'

'The council don't do naff all in Dullitch. The duke gets blamed for everything.'

'Nice,' Gordo said, nodding.

'Yeah,' Groan agreed. 'Seems fair.'

Tambor didn't like it when shadows fell across his drinking table, especially during the day. He lowered his head again and tried to examine the bottom of his tankard, but the shadow just kept lengthening.

'Oi, you. Come an' sit wiv us.'

Tambor looked up. He soon wished he hadn't; Groan Teethgrit was a sight to behold, but the man was probably not best viewed within the smoky depths of the Ferret. For a moment, Tambor thought he'd become the focus of attention for an angry mountain troll. Then he realized that, against all odds, the creature had spoken syllables (albeit fractured ones). And the face was familiar; Tambor had been an ordinary councillor during the Virgin Sacrifice Scandal, but there were some faces you simply didn't forget.

'I beg your pardon?' he ventured, desperately.

'I said, come an' sit wiv us.'

The murky giant pointed over to a table which was already playing host to a stocky dwarf and a boy who looked severely drugged.

'Um . . . I'm fine as I am, thanks.'

'How d'you mean?'

Tambor hesitated. 'Er . . . what I mean is, I'd quite like to go on sitting here, if it's all the same to you.'

'Right,' muttered Groan. 'An' I'd like a frog in a box, but we don't always get what we want, do we?'

Tambor managed a weak grin, picked up his drink and sidled over to the table. The muscled mountain loomed after him.

'Pull up a stool,' Gordo said, offering the elderly councillor a companionable smile. 'And tell us about this plague of yours.'

A sudden, all-knowing look came into Tambor's twinkling eyes.

'*Ah*,' he said. '*Now* I see. You're mercenaries.'

'An' you're a damn sorcerer,' boomed Groan, who'd taken offence. 'I can spot one a mile off.'

The councillor shrugged. 'I used to be back before the art was banned; a very good one too. Not any more, though. Now I'm in politics.'

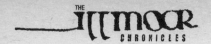

Gordo took a gulp from his tankard, and frowned. 'Don't you miss the life of adventure?'

'Desperately . . . but I suppose you can't throw fireballs forever. At least, not in this city. Hahahaha!'

'Yeah, so I heard. Any children?'

'None that'd admit to it. Got a grandson who talks to me, though; young Jimmy. He's a good lad, bit of an idiot, but you know how youngsters are these days. He works all hours of the day, waitin' tables down at Spews and scouting for the duke. I think he works of a night too, fetching stuff for people.'

'Ah, a noble trade,' said Gordo, tactfully.

'All thieves're scum,' said Groan, who'd heard of tact but hadn't bought any shares.

'I'll get rid of your plague.'

The table fell silent, and three pairs of eyes turned to consider Diek Wustapha. The boy looked momentarily electrified, then slouched forward and collapsed on to the table. Everyone looked at Groan.

'*What*? I didn't touch 'im.'

'Kids these days,' Tambor mumbled, shaking his head sadly. 'Drugged up to the damn eyeballs.'

It was fast approaching five o'clock.

The palace gates intimidated Oval Square, towering above nearby rooftops like the feet of a felled giant. At any other time of day guards would have been stationed there, but at weekends staff pressures triumphed and the walls had to take priority. This shouldn't have been a problem for an ex-sorcerer like Tambor Forestall but, like all the city's sorcerers, he'd been out of practice for some time. He spoke a few words in some secret, long-dead language and touched them lightly with his index finger. Nothing happened. He stared thoughtfully at the gates, waited for a whole minute then shook his head and gave them a damn good kick. He was about to make a second attempt when the light from the street lamp was replaced by a wall of chest and he suddenly found himself cast into shadow.

'Hurry up wiv those gates, will ya?' said Groan, an unconscious heap balanced on one shoulder.

Tambor shrugged.

'The gatehouse guards are a bunch of morons,' he said. 'They've forgotten about the mercenary reception and locked up for the day! I suggest we form a queue. I usually get noticed after five or ten minutes, even if I'm standing out here on my own. I'll ring the bell-pull; that helps.'

'Where is it?' said Groan.

'Over there, right hand side of the ga—'

'Fair enough,' interrupted Gordo. He marched over to the bell and yanked down hard on it. 'You're dealing with bloodthirsty mercenaries, here. We don't do queues.'

'He practically constitutes one on his own,' Tambor muttered to himself, scowling at Groan.

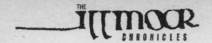

Gordo pointed up at his companion.

'If I were you, I'd dump that lad just inside the palace door. We've done him enough favours for one day. Besides, I reckon he can find his own way.'

The councillor smirked.

'He's no mercenary. Where's his sword?'

'He's bin hit on the 'ead or somethin',' said Groan defensively. 'Else he's high on magic. We found this on 'im.'

Groan pointed over to Gordo, who was waving Diek's flute.

'Ah, that explains it,' Tambor muttered. 'He's the charmer. Heralds say—'

He was interrupted by a loud clatter. Pegrand Marshall, Duke Modeset's belaboured manservant, was struggling up Palace Street laden with an assortment of bags and boxes. He stooped to collect them together, picked up the bundle, staggered a few feet and dropped them again. The party at the gate stood watching him with detached amusement.

'What's all this for, then?' said Tambor. 'Are we to take it that the duke is in residence?'

Pegrand nodded and kicked at a sack which had fallen from the top of the pile.

'The rats have driven him mad. He's thrown everyone out except the kitchen staff,' he said.

'I say!' Tambor gasped. 'That's not very sporting, is it?'

'He thinks it is,' Pegrand continued. 'And if you're going in there, I wouldn't keep harping on about the infestation. It's a bit of a sore point.' He cast a pained glance at Groan and Gordo. 'You'll be the mercenaries, then?'

They grunted a confirmation. Pegrand looked up at Groan's shoulder.

'Who's that?' he said. 'Another mercenary?'

'Don't think so,' said Gordo. 'Just a kid who charms folk with his flute. He's had a rough day.'

'Haven't we all? Can somebody help me with all this gear? I've got what feels like forty boxes of traps and those stairs are playing havoc with my back.'

They each took a few cases, and looped a rucksack over Diek's head. Pegrand produced a chain of keys and began the arduous task of finding the correct one.

'Remember to dump the kid,' Gordo said, striding through the gate and giving Groan a pointed glare as he passed. 'He's a damn nuisance.'

Tambor tucked his beard inside his robe.

'This'll be interesting,' he said.

Nine

The blackout subsided. It was strange waking up in a palace and not remembering how you'd arrived there, but it was even stranger waking up dazed and confused in a palace that looked as though it had been designed by a confirmed lunatic. The place was an absolute mess.

Cobwebs parted before Diek as he entered the kitchen. The staff consisted entirely of ghouls, hollowed grave-walkers who lurched around without purpose, stopping every few seconds to turn their empty eye-sockets towards vats filled with soup, which bubbled over, unattended.

Chickens squawked in cages, suspended on ropes from the kitchen ceiling. A dark-skinned wench with a flaking scalp brought down a chopper and severed one of her own fingers, which fell into a bowl of flour. She didn't look too surprised, though; perhaps it was part of the dish. Diek shook his head, wondering if the palace officials ever came down here. He hadn't seen so many dead people walking around since his grandmother's eightieth birthday.

Diek chose the section least occupied by zombies and sidled down it unobtrusively, careful not to draw attention to himself. On reflection, he decided that these people probably wouldn't notice an invasion, and moved on at greater speed.

The central passage wasn't much better. True, it wasn't full of the living dead, but it was full of Modeset family portraits which, though marginally more welcoming, were just as ugly. He fancied that he heard voices echoing far above so, stepping over a toppled bench, he cautiously ascended the stairs.

A little further up, he huffed on a pane in an arched landing window and peered out. Dullitch sprawled beneath the palace, a cityscape of rooftops and towers. So many people and – he paused to remember the words of the herald – three rats to every man. He had to be confident. *A confident demeanour is second only to a crystal clear mind, the perfect instrument for attracting faith in others.* Where did that come from? Diek shook himself from his reverie; he was beginning to feel unusually disorientated.

*

'Twice in one day,' said Tambor, puffing and panting as he conquered yet another flight of steps. 'I'll tell you fellows something for nothing; if I had my time again, I'd choose magic over politics and that's a fact. In my early days, I could've shot up here on a magic carpet.'

'You can't go up stairs on a magic carpet,' said Pegrand, still straining under his personal burden. 'It'd go on a diagonal and you'd fall off.'

'Well, I never fell off a magic carpet in ten years as a sorcerer and I'll be damned if I'd have fallen off one going up here.'

'It doesn't matter,' said Gordo, who'd seen an opening in the conversation. 'You fall off a magic carpet anywhere, you're stuffed. It's always a long way down unless you've just taken off.'

'Yeah,' said Groan.

Tambor scowled. 'Not if you were flying with old Wally Sprinkle. His take-offs were legendary. Birds used to migrate in accordance with his flight schedules.'

'Anyway, we haven't got one now,' said Gordo reasonably.

'Sometimes he didn't even need the carpet,' Tambor continued, mumbling to himself. 'Just used to take off on his own.'

To take his mind off the rat crisis, Duke Modeset had spent the afternoon searching for his current canine companion. He'd only seen the dog once since Pegrand had purchased it, and he felt a distant pang of guilt for the neglect. At least he'd found it now.

He was down on his hands and knees, peering into the darkness underneath the ducal throne. From what little he could see, it wasn't a patch on the Snowland Husky he used to own but it was a dog nevertheless, and was probably in need of care and attention. He wondered if it would like a biscuit.

The sound began even before Modeset had attempted to move away, a low-throated snarl that rose steadily in pitch and crescendoed into a growl bordering on insanity. Modeset found himself frozen to the spot in sheer terror.

Surely it can't be coming from the dog, he thought, keeping one eye on the curled-up fur ball under the throne. He suddenly realized that he couldn't tell which way the animal was facing. He was still speculating about it when an eye flicked open.

Even Diek heard the scream. It ripped through the palace; ornaments shattered, windows shook and latches rattled. He watched as a flock of birds erupted from the gardens and took flight. Then, just as suddenly, the sound faded away. All was silent.

Diek shook his head. He was beginning to realize that palaces were very strange places, especially this one.

*

Pegrand burst into the throne room and dropped his pile of luggage. The party of mercenaries and Tambor Forestall filed in behind him.

'Are you OK, milord?' he said.

The room appeared entirely empty. Pegrand looked to the left and right, then up at the ceiling. Eventually he looked down.

'What're you doing on the floor, milord?' he asked.

Modeset sighed.

'Practising my yoga, Pegrand. Would you be so kind as to pass me that marrow bone over by the door.'

The manservant motioned to Tambor, who rushed over to fetch the bone and handed it on, making sure to keep a fair distance between himself and the shape lurking under the throne. Pegrand tossed it at the dog, then helped the duke to his feet.

'That's Vicious,' said Pegrand.

'You're telling me,' said Modeset.

'No, milord. You named the dog Vicious, remember?'

'Oh, so I did. Quite right, too. Little bast—'

'THESE are the mercenaries, milord. You'll, er, you'll probably remember Groan Teethgrit and um—'

'Yes. Only too well.'

In what seemed like the blink of an eye, Modeset crossed the room and seated himself behind his pearly-white marble desk.

'Assemble!' he shouted.

Pegrand hurried around the room, ushering everyone

into a straight line or, at least, the nearest approximation of a straight line they could manage. Groan would've stood out on a map.

'Are these all the mercenaries we have?' Modeset asked.

Tambor thrust one hand into his robe and produced a tattered scrap of parchment. He squinted at it.

'A young man is unconscious downstairs. I believe he is this ... um ... how do you say it? I believe it's said Diyek, Diyek Wustafor,' Tambor managed, edging around every vowel as if it might suddenly leap out of the word and bite him.

'I see. Let's just leave him there for the time being, shall we? I'll deal with him later.'

Groan muttered under his breath, bumbled across the room and sat in the throne. Nobody in the room batted an eyelid, but Vicious took the opportunity to gnaw at the barbarian's ankles. It gave up after ten minutes.

Modeset had returned his attention to the councillor.

'Now if we can just—'

'I don't believe you'll have need of these men,' said a voice.

Tambor stepped aside to admit the young traveller, who marched over to the desk with an air of authority befitting a king. He treated the duke to a brilliant grin.

'My name is Diek Wustapha and I will rid your city of all unwanted guests for a far lower price than these mercenaries.'

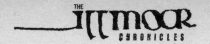

Gordo spat on to the mosaic tiles.

'How do you know?' he said. 'We haven't even quoted a price yet!'

'Don't take it personally, boys!' Tambor shouted. 'These yokels, they're all the same.'

'My methods will cause little civic unrest,' he continued, 'I'm sure we can come to some arrangement.' His voice had a strange, melodic tone.

Modeset looked from Diek to the mercenaries and back again. Then he steepled his fingers and used them to prop up his chin. A smile was forming.

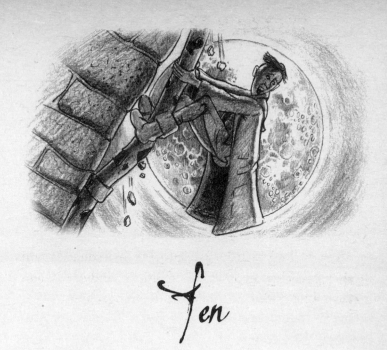

Ten

Tambor Forestall had never been one for company. He'd always preferred spending time by himself. It had nothing to do with the ancient adage about politicians being reclusive; he just didn't find people very interesting as a species. Besides, one mercenary guide-tour of the palace a day was enough for him. Bless the old sprout, they'd said under their breath. The cheek of it!

He stared down miserably at his hat, remembering his rare days of magic. He'd been through some hats in his time. He recalled, many moons ago, the apprentice deerstalker given to him on his arrival at the Velvet Tower in Legrash. Starting off as a lowly magician, he'd

then progressed through the ranks of sorcery: warlock, wizard, mage and, finally, sorcerer 1st class. He still couldn't help but feel, what with all the sniggering and sarcastic remarks, that it hadn't been worth it. To end your days as a councillor seemed more like a punishment than a pinnacle.

A tickling sensation in his foot made him lean back and peer beneath the tavern table. A small black rat was nibbling at the hole in his boots. He yelped, kicked it away and watched it scurry behind the bar. Then he inspected the boot. It was a pity the city council didn't upgrade boots, he thought to himself. He'd be on golden-hydes by now.

The Rotting Ferret's special performers for the evening were Farfl, Duk and Orfo, members of a cross-species band from Legrash. They were currently engaged in a heated dispute with Inky Mamaskin, master hypnotist, who claimed that their performances were sleep-inducing and therefore putting him out of business. Militia man Cedric Phelt was playing mediator. Phelt was a blunt, annoying, little man who put people in mind of a clockwork Punch. He stood amidst the feud like a pivot on a see-saw. Eventually the argument was settled, Inky took a seat and the trio got going. Phelt was nowhere to be seen. The remaining customers began to take the quick way out, some via the back door and some via the bottom of a bottle.

Tambor flicked through a heavy spell-book he'd

bought from a black market dealer in Birch Street. Apparently, it was one of the lucky few to escape being burned. He grinned, arriving at a few dusty pages near the back in which he'd already stashed some incidental notes. The volume was in good condition, and practically identical to his original one; Tambor felt sure the gods had meant him to find it.

'Excuse me?'

A dwarfish face smiled up at him.

'Mind if we join you again?' said Gordo, clambering on to a nearby stool without waiting for a reply.

Tambor wondered who the 'we' was and looked about him. Where once he'd had a clear view of the performance, now there was nothing but solid muscle. Then he remembered.

Groan removed his helmet and set it down on the floor beside his stool, disturbing a gang of rats who'd evidently come looking for the one Tambor had booted behind the bar. They soon moved when the helmet landed.

'What's happening tonight, then?' said Gordo. 'Enjoying yourself?'

'Not much,' said Tambor. 'But I was hoping to, after a few more of these.'

He turned his empty mug upside down on the table and belched.

Gordo shook his head, sadly.

'We've just travelled over land and, er, grass to save

this city from a major' – he paused – 'ratastrophe.' He nudged Groan in the elbow but got no reaction. 'And, d'you know what happened? Of *course* you do, the duke gave the job to a flamin' shepherd!'

'Doesn't surprise me a bit,' said Tambor, ignoring the accusation and staring gloomily at his upturned mug. 'City's run by ne'er-do-wells and bad politicians.'

'You're boaf, ain't you?' said Groan.

The sorcerer smirked humourlessly.

'One or the other,' he said. 'In practice it amounts to the same thing. One big chain. Oh sure, there's the council, but the city pretty well runs itself without too much hindrance from anyone but the duke.'

The band were on their fourth song. They had already outlasted the previous night's star turn, a troubadour who was still performing on a tempered spike outside the palace. At least, bits of him were.

'If I had four thousand gold coins,' said Gordo, 'I'd buy a little place of my own up in the mountains, with a horse and a duck.'

Tambor stared, bleary-eyed, around the room, a strangely sinister smile on his lips. The drink was beginning to get a foothold.

'Dofillidils,' he said. ' 'S what I want. A garden full of dofillidils.'

'I wouldn' 'ave any foreigners in my garden,' said Groan.

The dwarf glared at him.

'Who's that li'l fella over there?' said Tambor, pointing towards a corner table at the back of the room. 'He's smaller than you!'

Gordo tried to see where the old sorcerer was looking, in case there was a relative he could sit with. His gaze fell on a bright red hat with green flowers painted on it.

'That's a gnome, you silly old fool.'

Tambor blinked.

'Ah,' he said. 'What's the difference?'

'Dwarfs is bigger,' said Groan, to show he was paying attention. 'An' dwarfs 'as got beards, an' dwarfs is fatter an'—'

'All right!' Gordo snapped. 'I think he's got the point.'

'Why's he just sittin' there, then?' said Groan.

Tambor coughed over his beer mug and gave himself a froth moustache on top of his beard.

'P'raps he's got gnome to go to,' he said, and spent the next minute in quiet hysterics.

'May the gods help us,' said Gordo, looking out at the encroaching darkness. 'Look, we'd better start thinking about lodgings. We can't stay here all night and I'll be damned if I'm going back home without a brass nickel. The village Elders would have me in disgrace.'

'Then stay 'ere with me,' said Tambor, throwing one arm around Gordo and making a drunken attempt to get the other midway round Groan. 'My grandson's

comin' to meet me in a minute. He's a semi prof-proffec-proffectional thief. Gonna work for the Yowlers, he is. Best in the city.'

'Marvellous,' said Gordo, still hunting for a potential landlord among the bar's rowdy clientele.

In Dullitch, thievery was rife.

Some thieves would steal a gold tooth from a dying man, but only one would kill the man to get at the tooth. A thief so cunning, so malicious that he sought not only fame but also the theft of fame from others. A thief of random targets, of swift muggings in moonlit alleyways. In short, a thief almost entirely unlike Jimmy Quickstint.

Jimmy hung from the ceiling, three inches away from disgrace, the worst thief in the history of organized crime. The chandelier creaked. As he swung back and forth, legs constricted by the most inaccurate knot ever tied with two hands, he watched the glittering Shein Diamond roll across the carpet. A hairy Alsatian, who had been lying curled up beside the fire, trotted over, picked up the gem in its mouth and disappeared through an enormous archway in the west wall. It was the first time it had moved since he'd broken in. Animals had a sixth sense, they could detect danger in all its forms. This one had obviously decided it had absolutely nothing to worry about.

Jimmy looked up at the chandelier – just as the chord snapped.

It wasn't a great fall, but it was certainly an unfortunate one. Most of the room was carpeted but, as fate would have it, Jimmy landed heavily on a square of floor Lord Moffet had purposely overlooked when the money ran out. The chandelier landed on top of him. I should've been a beggar, he thought.

He heard someone approaching and strained to see who it was. The Alsatian, diamond still locked between its jaws, padded over to him. And lifted one leg.

'Where's that no-good grandson of mine?' said Tambor, who had passed through sobriety twice and was nearing the pint of no return. He'd never had so much fun involving other people before.

Chas Firebrand leaned over his shoulder and collected up three empty mugs, which he wiped around with the flap of his beer-stained apron and passed to the barmaid, a pretty young lass who had fluttered in earlier and caused Groan to pass out.

'What's he look like, this boy of yours?' said Gordo, checking Groan's pulse to make sure his friend was still breathing.

'Silly young bugger,' said Tambor. 'Got his father's face and his mother's walk – or was it the other way round . . .'

Chas frowned at the barbarian.

'Dear oh dear,' he said, shaking his head. 'He all right, is he?'

'Can't take his drink.'

THE
ittmoor
CHRONICLES

'Take mine,' said Tambor. 'Look after my drink, I do. Take mine right to the bladder.'

Chas winced.

'Blimey,' he said. 'That's some capacity you've got there, old man. You must be sweating booze.'

''S right,' said Tambor. 'Always swattin' beeze, me. Stripy bugs'll never know what hit 'em.'

Halfway along Tanner Street, Jimmy Quickstint stopped and kicked out at the nearest wall. Then he unfolded the night's remaining assignment and read:

> **Date**: Thursday 43rd Fortune, 1002
> **Assignment Location**: 14 Sack Avenue
> **Task**: Golden serpent-shaped idol
> **Objective**: Retrieval
> PLEASE INCINERATE AFTER DIGESTION

Jimmy had always wondered if the last bit was metaphorical. Did they really expect you to eat it first, then set light to it? Even multi-stomached Jobe Hanshaw would have his work cut out trying that. He read the note through twice before producing a tinderbox from the furthest reaches of his jerkin pocket and igniting the paper. Sack Avenue, eh? The Rich District, the Merchants' Quarter. He smiled to himself. This was it, his last chance to make it big. He would pass this assignment with flying colours and become Jimmy

84

Quickstint, first-grade Yowler thief. Well, not quite. He still had to perform some exclusive, never to be repeated, act of theft for his coursework, but an honours entry to the Runners proper did not come easy. You'd have to steal something truly amazing to pull that one off.

He replaced the tinderbox and headed up Tanner Street in the direction of Sack Avenue.

''S all about sex,' said Tambor, cheerfully.

Gordo tried to look away but the sorcerer was staring at him expectantly.

'What's that?'

'I said 's all about sex; life, I mean. When it comes down to it, they just don'tknowhowtoenjoythemselv—'

His head drooped forward.

'Thank the gods for that,' said Gordo miserably.

Evening washed over Dullitch, shrouding the city in a blanket of stars.

The crooked chimneys and myriad spires that made up the night-time silhouette of the rooftops were looking positively foreboding tonight. Down in Chapel Place the market traders were packing away for the evening, shuffling around their horse-drawn carts in a desperate attempt to fit everything in before the rain started. They were hampered in this pursuit by a large group of rats that were carrying out short but determined raids on each stall.

The Rich District had its own vermin.

Uptown, in the tree-lined avenues of the wealthy, a grappling iron hurtled over a high stone wall, failed to find purchase and quickly disappeared back over the top, accompanied by a yelp. A few seconds later it returned with increased momentum, landed on the roof of a stout kennel and was slowly and carefully retrieved until it caught firmly on to the collar of the biggest bloodhound in the Rich District.

In the darkness Jimmy smiled and gave the rope a few experimental tugs to ensure safety. It didn't give an inch. He reached a foot out gingerly and worked it into a crevice in the road-side of the wall, then he began to climb. A moment of confusion, caused by an unidentifiable scraping sound from the garden of the house, did little to halt his progress. He quickly pulled himself to the top of the wall, checked to make sure the sack was still fastened securely to his belt and promptly came face to face with the dog.

Despite its salivating jaws and snarling growl the animal was wearing a distinctly throttled expression, its eyes bulging grotesquely, as if trying to escape from its skull. After much soul-searching, Jimmy decided to try the front of the building instead.

Ivy seemed to be the general theme at 14 Sack Avenue; the three-storey concrete building was covered in it: from doorstep to chimneystack. It curled around the drainpipe and insinuated itself into every nook and cranny. A ladder had been left, rather carelessly, in the front garden beside an old (and similarly ivy-clad) well. Jimmy examined it critically and quickly recognized that it was useless for his purpose. It only had three rungs and one of those was propped up against a flowerpot some three feet from the ladder. Pathetic.

The only inspiring sight was a half-open window on the first floor. Cursing, Jimmy looked around for another means of entry but found none. There was nothing for it; he would have to scale the building unaided. As he tucked the small sack into a concealed third pocket he sensed, without question, that his entire future hinged on tonight's outcome. He had already lost his grappling iron (which he'd decided to let the dog keep) and clumsily broken a window. He briefly entertained the notion of grave-digging for a living.

Groan had recovered with alarming speed. He was now over at the bar chatting away to the barmaid, who smiled coquettishly and chuckled on cue. Gordo reflected that, when it came to women, Groan was never slow on the uptake.

Tambor, on the other hand, was out for the count. His head rested face-first in a plate of prunes he'd ordered on entering and had only got a quarter of the way through.

'Like her,' said Groan, returning to his seat with two giant mugs of something frothy. He dumped one in

front of Gordo. 'She said we could 'ave these on the 'ouse.'

The dwarf peered inside his mug, suspiciously.

'What's that red thing floating in there?' he asked.

'Em'royd, I fink,' said Groan. 'She's said her farver's bought himself a cherry orchard, on account of his trouble.'

Gordo took the statement on board but decided it was best left unravelled.

'Can I help you, sir?'

The voice shattered the silky silence of the night and Jimmy froze, absolute terror descending on him like a sack full of lead. He spun around to find a member of the City Guard, a wiry man of no height with a bulbous nose, looking up at him quizzically.

'No thank you,' he replied, tapping his foot on the ground in what he hoped was a nonchalant, carefree manner.

'It's just that, well, I can't help noticin' that you seem to be actin' somewhat suspiciously.'

'Ah, I see. Erm—'

'Are you a Yowler by any chance?'

'What, me? A cultist? No, sir! What an idea!'

'Well, what are you doin' in Lord Buckly's front garden, then, if you don't mind me asking?'

Jimmy's mind raced frantically for a plausible explanation. Unfortunately none occurred.

'I'm the gardener,' he said.

The guard continued to stare up at him, now sporting a look of vague incomprehension.

'Funny time to be gardening, isn't it? I mean, I've heard of—'

'I'm trying to find a special flower for his Lordship's indoor collection,' interrupted Jimmy, who was now talking too fast to think.

'Why can't you do that in the mornin'?'

'Because it's a special flower that only comes out at night.'

Strangely, this last explanation seemed to appear distantly plausible to the guard and he looked momentarily baffled.

'A nocturnal plant? Are you havin' me on?'

'No, it's true,' said Jimmy, knowledgeably. 'Usually they appear only in the Gleaming Mountains; "Phodo" they're called. "Phodo-Sithnisses".'

'Fair enough,' the guard said, nodding satisfactorily and turning to leave. 'Sorry to have bothered you.'

He stopped halfway towards the elderly wooden gateposts and turned around, a tired smile playing on his lips. He seemed to study the authenticity of Jimmy's ludicrous facial expression, before whistling in an awkward fashion and disappearing into the gathering evening mist. Jimmy sighed with relief and prepared himself for the climb. The only foothold attainable from a standing position came in the form of one of the

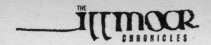
hinges that attached the drainpipe to the brickwork. He thrust his right foot hard between wall and iron and pulled himself towards his goal . . .

The creak came when he had reached the third hinge, just level with the landing window, the low, ominous grinding of century-old workmanship retiring. Jimmy tightened his grip on the pipe and prayed. Two minutes of grim silence later, he tentatively reached out a foot. With bated breath he swung his leg to and fro, gathering speed as the arc increased. Then, accompanied by only the slightest shriek of terror, he leaped through the air, finding purchase on the windowsill, where he hung, suspended like a rag doll, above the petunia patch. He hoped to the gods that the guard wasn't watching.

Jimmy scrambled frantically, his feet beating against the brickwork in a valiant attempt to relieve the pressure on his aching arms. Finally he managed to haul himself through the narrow window opening and slither into the room beyond.

Jimmy made a number of keen observations about the candlelit chamber he now occupied. The first was that the golden idol resting on a cushion inside an ornate glass cabinet standing against the east wall, was the one he was after. Then, in the following order, he noticed the lock on the cabinet door; the imposing four-poster bed with an elderly couple snoring away peacefully inside it; and, finally, the key fastened on the chain hanging around the sleeping old man's neck. In the silent shadows of that room, Jimmy discovered why the Rooftop Runners had just thirty-seven members. This situation looked, to all intents and purposes, impossible. How on earth was he supposed to retrieve the cursed key without waking the old boy?

Suddenly the figure lying next to the key-holder shifted uncomfortably beneath the blankets. Jimmy looked on in fascinated horror as the old woman sat up, swung her legs over the side of the bed and shuffled into a pair of bedroom slippers. Lord Buckly stirred in the throes of sleep, as his wife disturbed a number of creaking floorboards on her way to the door. Jimmy remained inanimate, a silhouette against the window. When the old woman had departed, he breathed a sigh of relief; perhaps luck favoured him tonight after all. It was as he considered his good fortune that a plan became clear to him. He crept forward, dodging the planks that the old woman had inadvertently indicated on her awkward journey a few moments before.

Hesitating to consider the implications should his plan fail, Jimmy climbed into the rickety four-poster bed and pulled the covers up over him. He remained perfectly still for a few seconds, pondering on how to advance his movement. Then, with lightning dexterity, he shot out a hand and snatched the key from its resting place on the old man's chest, looping it over his head and off in one swift movement that even Uole Twonk (the greatest thief in Dullitch history) would have been proud of.

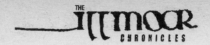

The key now in his possession, Jimmy lay panting on the bed with the satisfaction of success. He was about to climb out when a hand reached around his waist and grasped him tightly. At first he feared that Buckly had awakened, but then it became apparent that the old lord simply desired some after-midnight hospitality from his wife. The thief considered briefly what her Ladyship would do in this situation and consequently shoved the old man aside.

The key turned in the lock with an unnecessarily loud click and Jimmy snatched up the idol, which felt strangely sticky against his palm. Reaching down into his trousers, he pulled out the sack and tried, in vain, to slip the ornament inside. It wouldn't leave his hand. The vindictive old fool had daubed the piece with glue!

However, Jimmy had no time to revise his actions as Lady Buckly was now on her way back up the stairs, footsteps echoing loudly through the open door. Jimmy considered his drastic situation and dashed towards the window. He burst from the first floor of 14 Sack Avenue in a shower of glass and landed awkwardly in the petunia patch he had managed to avoid earlier. As screams erupted from the room above and various lights flicked on all over the Merchants' Quarter, a lone figure struggled to its feet and frantically kicked over a group of dustbins.

Unfortunately Jimmy didn't have time to snatch up the idol (which had fallen off, along with half the skin on his hand) before Lord Buckly's thirteen hounds bore down on him like the black plague of Armin Farris (a baker who produced some decidedly unhygienic bread).

'We can't leave until his grandson turns up,' said Gordo, indicating the unconscious Tambor with a nod of his head.

Groan looked puzzled.

'Why not?' he asked.

'Because,' Gordo began, wondering about the reasons himself. 'Well, it just wouldn't be right, that's all.'

The barbarian sniffed and downed his ale.

High above the streets of Dullitch, a shadow appeared. It danced along the rooftops, a strangely complicated gait that was either the result of sweeping skill, exhaustive training or categorical ineffectuality. Jimmy stopped to catch a breath and started; the stout pillar on which he was leaning turned out to be an unfinished stone statue of Juliette O' Rye-Nash, the celebrated priestess of Drygin, donated by the Alcoholic's Trust. It was missing an arm and two ears but, Jimmy reflected, it wasn't unusual for the society to leave a statue half-cut.

He dropped down a level, walked a little way with his back pressed firmly against a wall and arrived at the ledge edge. Problem. There was a considerable space

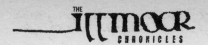

between the roof of City Hall and the roof of the Alchemist Museum. He looked down.

OK, he thought to himself. What are the chances of making a jump that big? Slim to none. Well, that's a relief. At least he wasn't trying to fool himself. Perhaps, if he timed the jump just right, he'd have a fifty per cent chance of making it to the other side. Trouble being, there was only a fifty per cent chance that he *would* time it right, so that left him back at square one.

Jimmy felt the first touch of rain on his cheek. His fingers, which had been groping frantically at the wall in case he lost his footing, found glass. He turned and peered through the window into a well-furnished office. He wondered how hard it would be to shatter the largest pane.

He held on to a fortunately placed carving above the portal, swung a leg back and brought his boot in hard against the glass. Nothing happened.

Far below in the street, a figure ascended the large flight of stairs that led to City Hall. A door opened and closed again. Jimmy didn't pay much attention.

I need more leverage, he thought. There was no way he could make a decent kick from this position. Jimmy shrugged inwardly. What was that old saying? If at first you don't succeed, try, try again. He swung back a second time, and two things happened. First the light came on and then somebody opened the window. Outwards.

*

'Oi,' said Groan, nudging Gordo's helmet with his elbow. 'You 'member that 'erald what met us on the road? He's jus' walked in.'

Jimmy had entered the Ferret and was in the process of apologizing to all and sundry as he bumped his way to the bar. He was covered in hay. Gordo watched as he stumbled up to Chas Firebrand and muttered something in his ear. Then he looked over in their direction and sauntered towards the table.

'That's my granddad,' he said, pointing at the unconscious councillor and smiling feebly.

'Aye,' said Gordo.

'Wanna make somefink out of it?' said Groan, who immediately took issue with anyone who began his sentences with claims of ownership.

'Nice helmet,' said Jimmy conversationally, nodding down at the battered looking piece of metal by Gordo's feet. 'Mind if I join you?'

'Sure,' said Gordo. 'Did you have a nice walk back?'

'Eh? Oh, yeah, thanks for that.'

The dwarf grinned.

'Sorry. No hard feelings. I'm afraid yer granddad here's the worse for drink.'

'He's piss'd,' translated Groan with satisfaction.

Gordo belched.

'Why are you all covered in that stuff?'

'Accident,' said Jimmy, smiling. 'Thank the gods for hay-carts, that's what I say.'

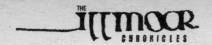

'Hmm . . . You know where we can get lodgings at this hour?'

'Well, there's always Finlayzzon's,' said Jimmy, thoughtfully. 'Or I s'pose I could sneak you in to the Runners HQ.' He looked wretched.

'No,' said Gordo. 'That first place you mentioned should be OK. Where is it?'

'On Stainer Street. 'S not far.' He sniffed and scratched his chin. 'Only, I wondered—'

'Yes?'

'Well—'

'What is it?'

'I don't suppose you could take Granddad with you?' He pinched one of Tambor's prunes and popped it into his mouth. 'Only, his landlady's a right old dragon and she's threatened to kick him out if he comes home under the influence again.'

'What?' Gordo exclaimed. 'But he's the council chairman, isn't he? Are you seriously telling me he hasn't even got his own house?'

Jimmy gave the dwarf a nervous grin.

'Politics doesn't pay you much of a wage in Dullitch,' he whispered.

Eleven

It was morning in Dullitch and a cool breeze bothered a dragon-shaped weathervane on the roof of the treasury. It spun around, whistled on the wind and broke off, embedding itself point-down in the sloping lower roof. A chimney-sweep, who had narrowly averted being impaled by leaping out of its path, fell six floors and crashed through a striped canopy over Stover's pie shop.

Duke Modeset smiled bitterly and turned away from the window.

'I hate this city, Pegrand,' he said. 'Well, maybe that's an overstatement, but I'm sure there are better places to rule. Ant hills, for example.'

'Ha! I don't care for it much myself, milord. I saw

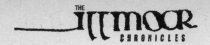

three trolls out on Banana Bridge yesterday, dangling a young lad over the side. It oughtn't to be allowed. Most of our citizens these days are petty crooks and vagabonds, milord.'

And worse, he thought. I'm not going to mention that dwarf with the butcher's daughter. He'd never seen such despicable behaviour.

'You're doing a fine job, Pegrand. Try to just relax and enjoy yourself. Think of this rat crisis as an extended vacation, albeit one taken at home.'

'How's that, exactly?'

Pegrand raised an eyebrow. There was definitely an emphasis on the word extended, and he wasn't sure he liked the implication. 'Surely you're not actually thinking of staying here during the attempted, er, rat out, milord?' he said, his voice edged with despair. 'Do you remember that idea you had a few months ago of faking your own death? Maybe this infestation is a blessing in disguise; an opportunity to leave this fleapit of a city to someone else. It's a terrible place, milord.'

'Yes, Pegrand, so you persistently tell me,' said Modeset. 'I'm sure I don't know *why* you continue to live here.' He's right, though, he thought; it is a complete and total dungheap. From its topmost tower to its deepest sewer. What was it that raggedy-bearded, kilt-wearing philosopher used to say? Ah yes: *beauty is only skin deep, but ugly goes right to the bone.*

He got down on his hands and knees and peered under the throne. Vicious was still curled up in a ball, growling softly in its sleep. He wondered what sex it was.

'Um . . . excuse me, gentleman.'

Modeset and Pegrand started. The Lord Chancellor, a thin and insipid man named Quarrell, stood beside the throne. He was attempting to shuffle through a collection of scrolls while standing up. Every few seconds a rogue parchment would slide off and drift away.

'I was thinking about the money situation, Duke Modeset,' he said.

'Oh yes?'

'Indeed.'

Pegrand sniffed haughtily and marched over to the window. He'd always despised chancellors, but Quarrell was definitely a snake in the grass if ever he'd seen one.

'Problems?'

'Well,' the chancellor continued, 'we've been experiencing some financial difficulties since the citizens stopped paying their taxes.'

Modeset's eyes narrowed.

'When was that?'

'About a year ago, sir. The shopkeepers still pay theirs and all small businesses donate a fixed sum per annum, but we've built up a backlog of debt with Legrash, you see, and—'

'Tell me,' Modeset asked, approaching the question with caution, 'exactly *what* do we have in the treasury, at this precise moment?'

The chancellor hurried over to the desk, snatched up a quill and did some rudimentary calculations.

'About—'

'Yes?' said Modeset, his eyebrows raised.

'Roughly—'

'Mmm?'

'Seven hundred and fifty-seven thousand, five hundred and twelve . . .'

Pegrand breathed a sigh of relief and even Modeset's death mask features experienced a second or two of astonishment.

'. . . sacks of Coral's Cut Price Coal.' The chancellor smiled weakly. 'A present from Baron Quaker of Legrash,' he added.

'Coal. I see.'

'Coal?!' echoed Pegrand. 'Suggest we hang this man, milord.'

'Silence. We'll do nothing of the sort.'

The chancellor exhaled.

'We'll let him explain it to the young man when he comes asking for his reward,' said Modeset. He smiled at Quarrell. 'I'm sure it's the very least you can do.'

'Certainly, Duke Modeset, it would be a pleasure.'

After all, Quarrell thought to himself, he's only a countrysider. What can *he* do?

*

When you're in the city, Diek's mother had told him, take a little time to stop and look around, drink in the beauty of it all.

Diek stood on the crest of Tor and stared down at Dullitch, sprawled across the landscape. It projected on to the Nasbeck Ocean like a dirty brown smudge. *Beauty.* The word rang in his ears. He stared for a long time, but couldn't seem to find any. *This is all just scenery, the crusty flesh covering an underworld of creeping darkness. It is your job to rid these people of their plague. Beauty is in the land itself . . . besides, none of that matters now. Now is your time. And so it shall be.*

He froze; the voice was worrying him now. Surely a conscience shouldn't sound that menacing?

Gordo had woken up in a few hellholes during his time, but he had to admit Finlayzzon's took some beating. It was more of a jail than a boarding house. Godrick Finlayzzon was a wealthy entrepreneur who had risen in status by thinking several steps ahead of his rivals and planning carefully for any anticipated complications. A grimy notice warned that guests would be locked in their rooms until they'd paid for the accommodation. In typical Dullitch style, the note was nailed to the *back* of the door.

'Can't you pay him?' Tambor snapped.

'Listen, you ungrateful sot,' said Gordo. 'Your

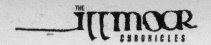

bungling dunce of a grandson got us all into this mess in the first place, so *you* can get us out.'

'But I haven't got any money!'

'Can't you conjure it open?'

'What, the door?'

'Yes, the door! Better still, *order* it open; you're head of the bleedin' council, aren't you?'

'Not any more,' Tambor murmured. 'I'm deserting.'

'You're what?'

'You've inspired me! I'm deserting the council for a life of magic and high adventure!'

'And yet you can't open a single damn door?'

'Nope; I, well, I left my spell-book at the Ferret.'

'And you can't perform a simple lock-picking without it? Some sorcerer you are.'

The dwarf stamped over to the window. Bars. You had to take your hat off to this Finlayzzon, he'd really thought of everything. Besides, it was quite a jump.

'Can't your barbarian wrench the door off?'

Gordo treated Groan to a doubtful look.

'Can you?'

The barbarian marched purposefully over to the door and gave it a determined kick. Some plaster cracked on the walls. 'Should fink so,' he said. 'Stan' back.'

Tambor had never seen a kick like it. Even Gordo gasped. The door flew out of the wall, taking the entire frame with it. Groan walked out into the hallway as if he was taking a morning stroll through the park. Gordo picked up his axe and beckoned to the old sorcerer, noticing how unstable the ceiling was beginning to look. Hairline cracks and patchwork crumbles sprouted along the east wall and the window dropped out, bars and all. The trio threaded their way along the corridor and down the stairs. Tambor made to leave a tip in the boarding house's Voluntary Contribution Box, remembered he didn't have any money, and stole a handful of loose change instead.

'Where're we off to now?' he called, hurrying across the cobbles to catch up with Gordo, who in turn was waddling quickly in order to keep pace with Groan.

'We?' Gordo snapped. 'What do you mean "we"? There is no *we*. There's only *us*.'

Tambor tripped over the scraggly ends of his robe and snatched at the dwarf's shoulder in an effort to regain his balance.

'Hey, I told you, I'm going back to a life of high adventure. I'm going to be a renegade sorcerer!'

'Yeah. So?'

'So, that's exactly what you need to complete your band.'

'We're not startin' a band,' Groan mumbled. 'We're mercen'ries.'

'Yes, well, you know what I mean.'

'Besides, I 'ate sorc'ry.'

'Ha! That's because you don't *understand* it.'

'All right then. You're in.'

Gordo stopped dead, and Tambor practically walked over him. Groan marched on a few yards, found he was talking to himself, and mooched back.

'What's up wiv you?' he said, looking down at the dwarf but avoiding eye contact.

'He's in?' Gordo exclaimed. 'Just like that? What happened to the Groan Teethgrit who won't have any truck with sorcery?'

'I just fort it might be good to have him wiv us, is all. In case we ever need a sorc'rer.'

'Thanks,' said Tambor, weakly.

'Are you serious? He can't even open a damn door!'

'That's not fair! I told you, I left my spell-book in the Ferret.'

'Well, you'd better go and get it, then. You're certainly no use to us without it.'

'Fine,' Tambor said, glaring back at the dwarf. 'I'll pick up my magic carpet as well. Are you coming?'

'Nah,' said Groan. 'Meet us at the gates in an hour.'

In the Ferret Jimmy Quickstint concentrated, fanned out his hand and flipped over the top card of the deck.

'Slipper!'

'That's never slipper!' shouted Chas Firebrand. 'You need a five or a twelve for slipper, you've only got three sevens.'

He snatched up the pack, shuffled and dealt again.

'I'm not letting you have another one on the slate,' he added. 'That's more'n twenty crowns you owe me.'

'No, I can't owe that much,' Jimmy protested.

'You do. Remember that stunt at closing time, last week?'

Jimmy tried to fake incomprehension.

'Er, don't recall exactly—'

'I bet you don't, my foot,' said Chas moodily, cracking his knuckles.

'OK, OK, don't get miffed,' said Jimmy. He slipped off his stool and collected a handful of mugs from the nearest table. 'There you go,' he added. 'Don't say I never do anything for you.'

Chas shook his head in disbelief and downed the remnants of his own ale.

'You know your problem?' he said.

'No. What?'

'You've got no sense of responsibility. I'm right, aren't I?'

'Could be, could be.'

'Take your granddad, last night. There he was, passed out over the table and who had to see that he got a decent night's kip? Two complete strangers. You didn't know them from Morris. They could've taken him into an alley and beaten him senseless. I bet you haven't even checked to see if he's all right; your own family. It's unthinkable.'

Jimmy closed one eye and cocked his head.

'He's an ex-sorcerer,' he said.

'So what's he gonna do, pull a rabbit out of a hat and hope it gives one of 'em a nip? Oh, and by the way, he left this here last night. If the rest of the council find out about it, he'll be thrown outta the city.'

Chas reached under the bar and produced a grubby, moth-eaten tome. The once gold lettering was faded, but Jimmy could just make out the word 'Grimoire'.

'That can't be good,' he admitted. 'I don't think Granddad knows that many spells as it is. Give it here.'

The thief stowed the book inside his jerkin, and without another word, hurried out of the tavern.

'Oi! What about my twenty crowns?'

Chas shook his head in disapproval, and pulled himself a pint. He was on his third gulp when Tambor appeared, puffing and panting, in the doorway.

'Chas, are you? All right? Is it? Spell-book. Left it, need it. Can I? Have?'

'You're about five minutes too late,' Chas said, downing the rest of his pint. 'Jimmy's got it. He's out there looking for you, now.'

'Of all the flkfjjdjs!'

'Cor blimey, is that orcish?'

'No, it's modern obscenity.' Tambor aimed a kick at the door, and missed. Then he turned and headed out on to the street. 'Tell Jimmy I'm leaving Dullitch,' he called back.

'You what?' Chas yelled. 'Since when?'

'This morning! I'm joining a band of bloodthirsty mercenaries. To hell with you all! Hahahahahah!'

Elsewhere in the city trouble was brewing . . .

It began as the merest hint of a tremor, a ripple in the water-bowl of audibility. Some dust drifted between ceiling and floor in a cellar beneath the Ackerman fishery. Vicious pricked up half an ear. The sound was distant, almost lost on the wind. It teetered on the brink of existence . . . and began to rise.

Rumble.

'Pegrand?'

Rumble.

'Milord?'

Rumble.

'Is that your stomach?'

Rumble.

'No, milord. I thought it might be yours.'

Crash.

Outside, atop the Crest Hill, Diek Wustapha played his terrible melody, while far above him lightning cast a net of electric veins across the sky. For the few folk abroad on the streets lucky or, depending on your view, *unlucky* enough to witness the music, its tune shifted in and out of audibility, high and low, thunderous and harmonic. For the briefest of moments, they were captivated. However, the real captives were the rising, swelling waves of rats that appeared from the basements

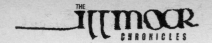

and the gutters, knitting together and tumbling towards the lure.

A door burst open somewhere in the southern half of the city. A woman screamed. Nothing happened for a whole minute. Then she was joined by others. Windows were flung open. People rushed out into the streets. A few of the braver citizens were attempting to get a good view of the episode by climbing out on to the rooftops and negotiating precarious slopes filled with damaged slates. Everyone wanted to see what was causing the uproar.

Diek Wustapha was strolling calmly through the streets, a merry melody rising from the flute he raced back and forth between his lips. He had a miniature city-issue map in one hand and stopped at various junctions, regarding it critically.

He was noticed by a couple of citizens on Market Street, not for the fact that he was playing a tune, but because he was seemingly oblivious to the kerfuffle erupting all over the city.

A rat emerged from the open cellar of a tavern in Stainer Street as Bakeman's Brewery Cart unloaded a barrel of ale. It was followed by others, a dozen, a score and a hundred or more. Then a multitude, a million, a mischief.

They swarmed between the houses, piling over one another to reach the magical music. Some were as tiny as mice, some were as large as kittens. Some were cute and cuddly, some were disfigured monstrosities. They needed the melody, yearned to reach it, scurrying faster and faster past streets whose inhabitants stood frozen in their wake. On and on they went, scrabbling with greater urgency at every turn.

'Will you look at that!' Chas Firebrand spat, leaning against the door of the Ferret. 'He's taking the rats! Unbelievable! Criminals in this city, they'll steal anything!'

He saw a flurry erupting from his own cellar.

'Oi!' he shouted, to no one in particular. 'I want a crown each for those.'

'Hey,' called a passing beggar. 'Are you insane? He's doing us all a favour.'

'Hah! Not me; I likes rats, I do.'

The beggar shook his head in amazement.

'Yeah, well,' he managed. 'There's always one, isn't there?'

At the mouth of an alley just off the corner of Stainer Street and the Goodwalk, Malcolm Siddle stood on the back of the Grim company cart and stared in amazement as the sea of vermin swept past.

'Here, Mr Grim,' he shouted. 'What d'ya think of all this?'

His superior watched as the last of the seething horde rounded Stainer Street and disappeared.

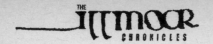

'Well, that's us out of a job,' he said.

The gates of the city slammed shut and there came a resounding hum. Then there was nothing but ear-splitting silence.

'I hope we have all learned a valuable lesson from this,' said Duke Modeset, from the battlements of Dullitch Palace. 'If you want a job doing properly, always go out into the countryside and find a simpleton to do it for you.'

Pegrand and Chancellor Quarrell nodded.

'I think that's the last we're likely to see of our furry friends,' he continued. 'But not, I expect, the last we've seen of the great Wustapha. He, of course, will be coming for his money.'

Pegrand sneered and sidled away. Modeset turned to face the chancellor and smiled humourlessly.

'I told the young man he could collect his reward from the treasury, Mr Quarrell. I trust you've thought of a believable excuse?'

He got no reply.

Twelve

Six miles out from Dullitch, Diek Wustapha stood on a narrow wooden jetty that extended into the Winter River and watched the first of the rats plummet to their doom. A few cunning exceptions managed to shake off the hypnotic melody long enough to swim for the shore, but a terrible, unseen force pushed them back until they too sank beneath the surface of the water. Diek felt a detached sorrow for them, but he was far too worried about other things to sympathize.

Where did the tune come from? He had little notion. Indeed, he couldn't even remember consciously making a decision to offer his services. It just sort of happened, spontaneously. Come to think of it, he was only dimly

aware of having left for Dullitch in the first place. The whole episode was like some strange dream, complete in every detail without need of his mental application. He was experiencing an icy calm. The voices had gone. He didn't know whether this made him feel better or worse.

The rats continued to roll over one another, careering towards the icy embrace of oblivion.

Far off to the west, a storm was brewing. Grey clouds gathered over the Varick Pass. Diek shivered and pulled his cloak tight around him. Then he looked back in the direction of Dullitch . . .

. . . where the sun was disappearing between clouds heavy with rain. It was one of those days that just couldn't make up its mind. In the palace . . .

'I was thinking,' said Modeset, 'about something along the lines of "finders keepers, losers never stray".'

'I think you've got a bit mixed up there, milord,' said Pegrand thoughtfully.

'Well, whatever, it's the principle of the thing. He bails out when the fire gets hot, I don't see why I should burn down my own kitchen.' Modeset blinked. That definitely didn't sound right.

'Are we still talking about the foreigner, milord?'

'No, no, no! I'm talking about the chef. I fired him this morning. He's the worst one we've had yet, him and those wretched zombies he has working for him.

It's like a morgue in that kitchen. The gods only know what drops off them when they're cooking.'

'Erm, yes, I see, milord. If I might change the subject, we haven't heard anything from young Wustapha yet.'

'And?'

'Well, I just wonder what he's done with all those rats.'

'Who cares? As long as they are out of Dullitch, they're somebody else's concern.'

'Let's just hope he's not taken them to Legrash, milord. Otherwise we might have to give back some of that coal.'

Modeset smiled.

'Dear, dear friend,' he said. 'Always the thinker, eh?'

'Whenever I'm given the initiative, milord.'

The duke regarded Pegrand out of the corner of one eye. Everything the man said was double-edged. He could make simple phrases such as 'Good morning' or 'Tea, milord?' sound like part of a countrywide conspiracy. He wondered if there was a man like Pegrand behind every great leader in Illmoor history. A man you didn't feel too comfortable about standing in front of. A man with a grin which said 'After you, milord.' Modeset swallowed. It was a sobering thought.

*

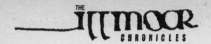
The following morning, there came a thunderous knocking on the doors of the Treasury. A panel slid open.

'Yeah?'

Diek stared at a face. It wasn't a particularly nice face. In fact, it only qualified for membership within society because it had all the correct bits. Diek couldn't even put a race to it.

'My name is Diek Wustapha,' he said, authoritatively. 'I have come for my reward.'

'Hold on,' said the face and disappeared into the shadows.

After a minute or so, it returned.

'No can do,' it said. 'My orders say you've got to go see the chancellor.'

'Is that right? And where would I find him?'

The panel slid shut, and there was some whispering. Then it shot open again.

'Follow the alley round to the back of the Treasury. There you'll find a small door with a gold plate next to it. Knock three times for the chancellor's secretary.'

Diek waited for a time, expressionless. Then he turned and walked around to the alley.

The chancellor's secretary was a man of few words, and he looked positively resentful even to let *those* go.

'Sit,' he snapped. 'Wait.'

Just over an hour later, Diek was admitted to the chancellor's inner sanctum.

Quarrell was seated behind his desk, both hands flat on the tabletop and a faint smile playing on his lips.

'Welcome, Mr Wustapha,' he said. 'Any problems?'

'None whatsoever,' said Diek, his eyes narrowing to slits. 'I understood that I was to collect my payment from the Treasury. When I arrived there, I was told you wished to see me beforehand. So I'll ask you the same question you just asked me: are there any problems, chancellor?'

There was something in the boy's voice that Quarrell was quite certain he didn't like one little bit. It had undertones in it. He was sure countrysiders shouldn't have voices with undertones.

'As a matter of fact, Mr Wustapha,' he said, 'there is.'

'Oh?'

'Before I go into all that,' Quarrell went on. 'I must ask you: what did you do with the rats?' He crossed his fingers under the table.

'I drowned them,' said Diek, a sudden flash of concern showing on his face. 'You didn't want them back, did you?'

Quarrell's grin could have melted lead.

'No no, of course not,' he said. 'We just wanted to be certain that our plague would not return to, well, plague us.'

'There's little chance of that,' Diek said, without rancour. 'Now, where are my thousand crowns?'

Quarrell's eyes widened.

'Goodness gracious,' he exclaimed. 'Is that what the good duke told you? A thousand crowns? For sweeping out a few rats?'

Diek's face remained expressionless. But deep inside his mind, the voices were returning.

'*Is that your final word, chancellor?*'

'I beg your pardon?'

'*You have no intention of paying me what I'm owed? Is that your final word?*'

Quarrell started. He was beginning to get the feeling that he'd missed the middle of the conversation. His fears weren't calmed by Diek's sudden smile or by the icy glaze over his eyes.

'I'm sorry,' he managed. The room became silent, a dark, brooding quiet that was more unsettling than a hundred heated disputes. Quarrell felt something else was required from him. 'We haven't the funds to pay you,' he added.

'*And you knew this when you set me to the task?*'

'Yes.'

'*I see. Thank you, Chancellor Quarrell.*'

Diek said nothing more. He simply rose from his seat, opened the door and strode out into the hallway. The portal closed with a decisive click.

*

'What do you mean "gone"?' said Jimmy Quickstint.

'All three of 'em together,' said Finlayzzon, 'just before the rats left. They wrecked the joint on their way out, I might add. *And* they robbed my donation box; how low can you sink, eh?'

He waited to see if there was any emotional reaction from the lad.

'Well?'

'Well what?' said Jimmy. 'You don't expect *me* to pay for them, surely?'

Finlayzzon shrugged.

'You said you were a relative.'

'Yeah, I am,' said Jimmy. 'The poor relation.'

'Ah . . . pity.'

'Yes, it is. Now, do you have any idea where they went?'

Finlayzzon shook his head.

'Thanks,' said Jimmy. 'I'll make sure to point all my friends away from here in future.'

'Good!' Finlayzzon called after him. 'At least it'll keep the thieves out.'

Diek stumbled through the streets, his head swimming with rage and confusion. The crowds swarmed around him. So much noise and so many people. *But you know another tune, don't you, Diek?* He stopped, looked around and grabbed the arm of a passing juggler.

'What did you say?' he asked.

The man looked bewildered, shook himself free.

'Here,' he said. 'What's your problem, mate?'

Diek shook his head.

'You're nuts, you are,' said the juggler, taking a few steps back and colliding with an old woman selling herbal remedies.

You know another tune, Diek.

'Shut up!'

And a place, a magical limbo for traitors.

'Stop! Go away!'

A crowd of spectators was widening around him.

Play the other tune, Diek, the voice went on, *they deserve it. There is a place, a secret place of which I am aware. Take your revenge and I can lead you there. No one will ever find them, Diek. No one will ever find them . . .*

Thirteen

Night arrived in Dullitch unfathomably fast. It was a great source of concern for lateral thinkers, who couldn't find an eclipse-shaped loophole in their logic. Perhaps, they reasoned, it had something to do with Interstellarized Fog, before holding their hands up and admitting that they'd invented that one because it sounded authentic.

A single light flickered in the topmost tower of Dullitch Palace. Duke Modeset was scribbling. It was something he'd done ever since he was a boy, whenever he'd had trouble sleeping. He'd take a quill and a clean scrap of parchment and scratch down all his thoughts; get them out into the open, as it were. Then he'd take

them along to a telepathic in town where the underlying message would be unravelled. Usually it was something like you needed more greens or a prune or two in the morning to keep your bowels open.

Modeset put down the quill and started; he'd drawn a rat. This was turning into quite a fixation. It was the same reason he'd had trouble sleeping, visited in the small hours by nightmare scenarios which had him sprinting across desert wastelands, pursued by seething hordes of rodent marauders. And Diek Wustapha. The countrysider had been out in front, producing terrible melodies without need of any kind of instrument. They just sort of emanated from him, as if he had a gland for producing harmonics.

Modeset shivered. This was ridiculous. Besides, he'd come to a decision: it was time to abdicate. As soon as the war with Phlegm was won, assuming it *could* be won (assuming, in fact, that anyone from Phlegm actually realised that they were involved in a war) and the furore from the rats had died down, he was off. Somewhere. Anywhere. Soon. Ten years was quite enough. Dullitch was far too strange a kingdom, especially at night. Weird screams would erupt from nowhere, hideous twisted cries of people facing horror without mercy. Modeset was beginning to recognize some of them by pitch. The low, continuous moans were usually the Burrow Street Trolls leaping out on some poor, unsuspecting beggar. While the higher wailings were caused by young ladies running into Jock the Toddler (a fiend who stalked the streets of Dullitch after sundown, preying on certain types of women. He hadn't actually murdered anyone, but a greengrocer's wife had some nasty nips on her ankles).

A door slammed somewhere off to the east. Modeset crossed to the arch windows and peered out into the murky midnight gloom, but he couldn't see very far in front of his hands for the fog. A second door slammed, followed by a third and a fourth. He sniffed. Perhaps it was a contest. This city had some curious idiosyncrasies; it wouldn't surprise him. He produced a woolly hat from his robe pocket, took up his candlestick and wandered down to the dungeons.

Only two of the cells below Dullitch Palace were occupied. The first contained Elee Klias, a geriatric old woman who muttered constantly on the subject of vintage wines and the encouragement of nudity. Presumably, old Duke Culver had imprisoned her for the latter. After all, you could excuse public shouts of 'Weedles' Red' but there was no getting around 'show us your floppy mushroom'. Modeset ignored her incessant whining and went straight to the second cell.

As he flung open the door, his frame illuminated a pillory inside of which struggled a trembling figure. Modeset used his candle to light three further brackets before turning to face the small, wizened face of Rochus the Soak.

'Evening, seer,' Modeset said calmly. 'How are they treating you down here?'

Rochus coughed and spluttered.

'Thou shalt pay for this . . .'

'Really? An unfortunate attitude, for you were to be released tomorrow.'

'Ha! Empty words; I've never encountered such insolence in my life.'

'Mmm?'

'You'll swing from the yard-arm for this.'

'Oh, do be quiet, man! Surely you're not still under the delusion that you're some kind of god?'

'I am a great deity, like my father before me.'

Modeset tried to invoke images of Anglucian the Soak. From what he could remember, the man had been a notorious womanizer, but had little to boast about in the evangelic department. A reputation for scampering across battlements pursued by furious husbands didn't exactly paint a portrait of unearthly nobility. Furthermore, Modeset found it difficult to recall ever seeing the Great Soak with his britches on.

'Well, now that you mention it—'

'Silence! Your lips seal your doom.'

'How amusing,' said Modeset. 'Tell me, are you going to give me the information I require voluntarily, or am I going to have to take another set of pins to your fingernails?'

This question caused Rochus to lapse into a choking fit.

'So, great scryer,' the duke continued, raising his eyebrows. 'What is going on in my decrepit city? A single word will suffice, as long as it's accurate. Conspiracy, perhaps? Some devilish form of rodent warfare from Legrash?'

Rochus's cracked lips trembled, parted.

'M-m-magic,' he said. 'Dark, terrible magic.'

Modeset nodded, rose. As he closed the dungeon door, the soak began to cry.

'Show us your winter warmers!' screamed Elee, from the next cell.

Midnight loomed . . .

A short distance from Dullitch, Gordo Goldeaxe sat beside a small campfire and gnawed his way through a chicken leg. Groan and Tambor were sleeping and, despite the fact that their combined snore could have penetrated the eardrums of a man some sixty miles away, Gordo wasn't paying them any undue attention. This was because, for the last half an hour, he had been watching a vast cloud form over the city. It was a magical cloud, he felt sure, because it crackled with energy and glowed alternately white and purple against a backdrop of darkness.

It was also very, very unsettling. Gordo had heard about such atmospheric oddities, of course, and how

they formed in an area where gargantuan amounts of magic were being used, but something about this particular build-up was making him wish he'd taken first watch of the evening.

The screams started just after sunrise, and again Modeset put them down to good, old-fashioned Dullitch eccentricity. It was only when he came downstairs for breakfast that he realized things were a little more serious. As he descended the small flight of steps leading to the Great Hall, an entourage of city officials alighted on him like vultures on a corpse. Pegrand was nowhere to be seen.

'They broke down my door!' yelled Quaris Sands, the Home Secretary, above the fray.

'They've demanded we hang you, Duke Modeset!' added another voice.

Pegrand appeared at the doorway, rushed inside and slammed the portal.

'There's a rabble outside, milord,' he shouted. 'It looks like half the city.'

Modeset raised his hand for silence; to his surprise it worked.

'One at a time,' he began, offering the group a reassuring smile. 'Pegrand, why is there a rabble outside?'

'It's that countrysider, milord,' said his manservant. 'Three beggars saw him on Stainer Street and—'

'Doing what?'

'Taking the children.'

Modeset frowned.

'What, all of them?'

'Yes, milord. In the night, like a thief.'

'But, how?'

'Same way he got the rats, by all accounts. Played a tune and they followed him.'

'And the militia man on duty?'

Pegrand swallowed.

'Chap named Phelt, milord,' he said breathily. 'He fell asleep. I think he'd been drinking.'

'I see,' said Modeset, turning his attention to the rest of the group. 'You, with your hand up, you wish to say something?'

Quaris Sands nodded.

'I'm afraid that the Yowler Churches, as well as several other religious establishments, have issued statements condemning the situation. If matters are not put in order by Friday, there will be repercussions.'

'I see.'

'I wouldn't have bothered you with it, milord. But what with the Church of Urgumflux the Wormridden being practically next door—'

'Yes, yes. Does anybody else have something to contribute?'

'I do,' said Chancellor Quarrell. 'Understandably, people are beside themselves with distress and

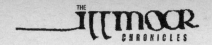

confusion, however there is a third party inciting them to riot.'

'A third party?'

'Yes, milord. A young lad came back on his own, said he'd been under the musical spell but he hadn't been fast enough to keep up with the rest. He's lame in one leg, you see.'

'Hmm . . . interesting. Did he happen to see where the foreigner was headed?'

'Not really, milord. I mean, only the direction . . .'

'Right, and can we make any guesses based on that?'

'A few; there's not many places he could take them without passing one of the villages, and we'd have heard already. Of course, there's a lot of forest out there, and mountains, I'll grant you.'

'Hmm . . . your guess, Mr Quarrell?'

'Well, if it was *me* – not that I'd kidnap a load of kids—'

'Of course not.'

'Of course not, but if I *did*, and I wanted to get a ransom or something, I'd go for one of the mountains. Lot of blind spots, see, caves and such. You could hide an army up there. Mind you, Great Rise is a good day and a half away, so I'd hedge bets against *that*. The Twelve is nearer.'

'Right, at least we've got a few possibles to go on. Now, about the boy, doesn't it seem strange to you that this lone youth returned unscathed?'

Quarrell took a deep breath.

'Apart from the leg, you mean?'

'Ha! He had that before.'

'Well, I just don't think . . .'

There was a disapproving murmur from the gathered officials, but Modeset forged on, regardless. 'So there's the chance of a conspiracy between the boy and the foreigner?'

'Um . . . no . . . not unless you think he's inciting a riot, milord.'

The duke's smile spread like treacle.

'Exactly! You see? Now you know what to suggest. I'll watch out for this boy during your speech.'

'M-m-my speech?'

Modeset clapped his hands together and motioned to two of the palace guards. They marched into the fray of city officials and each snatched one of the chancellor's arms.

'Pegrand,' the duke went on. 'Have a scroll nailed to every notice-board in the city. There's to be a public announcement and,' he smiled, 'a public execution. Mr Sands, assemble the council and prepare a statement to satisfy every parent in Dullitch that their children will be returned.'

Modeset peered over a collection of muttering heads.

'I'll have my breakfast now, Pegrand,' he added.

The diamond clock on Crest Hill chimed eleven.

Quaris Sands, who'd had to stand in for Tambor

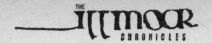

Forestall when the chairman had failed to arrive, shuffled a ream of parchments and leaned forward across the table. From what little he could make out through strobes of piercing sunlight, only a percentage of the council had bothered to turn up.

'Right,' he began.

'Go on . . .'

'Well . . .'

'Yes?'

'The fact is . . .'

'What?'

He narrowed his eyes at the troglodyte translator, whom he'd patiently observed at the last meeting and who now looked like something crossed between a goblin and a bowl of suet. Its long warty nose still dripped a horrid mucus which burned holes in the new oak table and smelt acrid. Quaris stared around the room and noticed that the orc representative was absent. Shuffling through his minutes, he found a glare to reflect the situation and turned it on the troglodyte.

'Where's that fella you're translating for?' he asked. 'There's no point in you being here if he's not present. You might as well disappear.'

The troglodyte smiled. 'I'm part of the council now, official like. I joined yesterday.'

Quaris shook his head at the little creature.

'You can't be a member,' he said.

'The duke's secretary seemed to think I could,' said

the translator, holding something under Quaris's nose.
'He gave me this scroll. It's signed and everything.'

'So it is. '

'So I'm a member now, right?'

'It would appear that is the case.'

'My mum'll be proud. She always wanted me to go into
politics. I remember when I was little she used to say . . .'

The chairman closed his eyes and prayed for patience.

'Right,' he said. 'I'd like to call to order the, er, latest
meeting of the Dullitch Council. We're gathered here
today –'

'Sounds like the start of a funeral,' said the translator.

'– to compose a speech for Duke Modeset to address
to the citizens of our fair city.'

'That's going to be tricky.'

'I wonder if I may make a suggestion,' said Taciturn
Cadrick.

Everyone stared at him expectantly.

'Perhaps,' he continued, 'we could blame
transdimensional demonics.'

A collection of blank faces gave not the merest
indication of understanding.

'That is to say, the infringement of demons into our
civilized society. Something very similar happened a
while back, when I was Trade Minister for Legrash.'

'What's that got to do with kidnapped children?' said
Quaris, with a frown.

'Quite a lot, actually' – he took a deep breath – 'I

believe that Diek Wustapha has been possessed by a despicable demonic fiend.'

This didn't engender quite the reaction he was expecting.

Quaris grimaced.

'A show of hands for Mr Cadrick's suggestion?' he ventured.

Two went up, and they both belonged to Taciturn.

'Right,' said Quaris. 'Then that's firmly voted out. Anyone else?'

'How about this,' said the translator, rummaging in a satchel beside his stool and producing a roll of parchment which he then proceeded to unravel. 'Citizens of Dullitch. There has been a terrible catastrophe but I, your duke, and the honorary members of your City Council have come up with a solution. We have dispatched a hunting party to find the stolen children and bring this terrible fiend to justice.'

Quaris opened his mouth and closed it again.

A few members at the other end of the table clapped their hands in approval. Taciturn Cadrick rested his chin on his hands and tried to look miserable.

'Excellent,' Quaris managed. 'Where did you say you were from?'

'I didn't,' said the translator, his candlewax nose disgorging another globule of mucus. 'And, besides, it's not perfect. For a start, we don't *have* a hunting party.'

An air of gloom settled over the table.

Taciturn Cadrick was the first to speak.

'How about that barbarian fellow in the Rotting Ferret the other night, with the dwarf?'

'No,' said Quaris firmly. 'They came at the city's request and we told them to get lost. They're hardly likely to help us now and, besides, they've probably left already. They could be miles away.'

Taciturn shook his head.

'Pity. They had our chairman with 'em too.'

'Tambor?'

'Yes.'

'Tambor Forestall was socializing with mercenaries?' gasped Quaris, as if the very thought was abhorrent to him.

'Absolutely, and he got a fair bit of ale down him I'd say. In fact, I think I heard Chas Firebrand say something about him leaving the city with them.'

'Well, that's fantastic,' Quaris snapped, glaring at the Trade Minister with naked distaste. 'How unutterably superb! Our chairman has run off to join a mercenary band. That's just rosy, isn't it? Does anybody actually feel like pretending to be a member of the council, you know, just for the afternoon?'

He turned to the troglodyte translator.

'What did you say your name was?'

It shrugged.

'Burnie.'

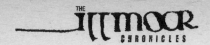

'Burnie,' repeated Quaris. 'Send a message to the Rooftop Runners. I wish to speak with a young man called Jimmy Quickstint.'

Three hours later, Duke Modeset sat in the throne room of Dullitch Palace and gazed down at an exhausted Quaris Sands.

'You really must do something about those stairs, milord,' the acting-chairman managed between puffs. 'I can't see me lasting long in my new post if I keep having to mission it up here every afternoon.'

'I didn't *build* the palace, Mr Sands,' Modeset pointed out. 'And I certainly don't have enough money to call in the stonework beauticians.'

'Ah yes . . . um . . . humble apologies, but I think they're called Masons.'

'Whatever. You have my speech?'

'Indeed. And a progress report, my lord.'

The duke raised one eyebrow.

'It appears that we have in fact formulated a plan,' Quaris fought on.

'Really? How splendid.'

'Yes. We, that is, the council, have decided to send a hunting party after the villain.'

'A hunting party?' The duke smiled. 'How traditional.'

Quaris nodded.

'A powerful sorcerer who, until recently, was in fact, um, a city dignitary and, um, hopefully, the two mercenaries you met yourself. There's only one problem,' he added.

'Which is?'

'They've already left the city. We've found the, um, *sorcerer's* grandson: he's a trainee member of the Rooftop Runners. He thinks they may still be on the Dullitch road, and he's agreed to go after them and ask for help.'

Modeset scratched his chin thoughtfully.

'So, in point of fact, we have hired a hunting party that doesn't yet realize either that it is hired or that it *is* a hunting party. Splendid work. By the way you're staring at your feet, I assume there is a problem even with this pitiable lack of a plan?'

'Well, as you say, milord,' Quaris went on, 'the problem is that they're bound to ask why the Wustapha lad kidnapped the children and when Jimmy, that's the grandson, tells them it was because you didn't pay him, they're hardly likely to trip themselves up in a rescue attempt, are they, milord?'

The duke relaxed, flexed his arms and offered Quaris a wry smile.

'Not a problem, Mr Sands. When does this "Jimmy" leave?'

'In approximately' – Quaris stared out of the eastern arch towards the diamond clock on Crest Hill – 'one hour.'

'I see. Then give him this to take with him.'

Duke Modeset rose purposefully, marched through a door in the north wall and reappeared carrying two

small but heavy-looking pouches. He tossed them to Quaris and went back for another two.

'There's over a hundred crowns in each pouch,' he said. 'They'll get a further five hundred each if and when they return the children unharmed, having disposed of this young freak.'

'May I ask where all this money came from, milord?'

'Certainly,' said Modeset. 'The good chancellor was looking after some of it for the greater prosperity of the city.' The sun played over the Royal Crest. 'In a room above the Silversmiths on Furly Lane,' he added.

'I'll make sure the boy gets going as soon as possible,' said Quaris.

'Can we trust a thief with the city's entire gold reserve, do you think?'

'I don't think we've got much choice, Duke Modeset.'

'Quite right. Let's just hope Quarrell's execution will satisfy the crowd. Oh, and Mr Sands?'

Quaris hesitated at the door, turned and raised an eyebrow. 'Milord?'

'This dignitary turned sorcerer ... it wouldn't be Tambor Forestall, by any chance?'

'Oh no, er, um, no, my word, absolutely not...'

'That's a yes, then, is it?'

'I'm afraid so, my lord.'

'I feared as much. You are excused, Mr Sands.'

Quaris muttered something unintelligible under his breath, and ambled off.

Fourteen

Charcoal clouds gathered over the Varick Pass, hung there motionless for a time and then began to spit all over the place like the worst kind of wine-taster.

Low-lying formations encircled the tallest peaks. It was said that, upon reaching the summit of the Twelve, a man could be forgiven for thinking that he had entered a land of balding giants. Patches of sparse woodland dotted the mountain-sides, home to a few of the region's more unsociable dwarf tribes and frequented by trolls, ogres and the occasional wandering Nojusyeti (a mythological beast with elongated feet, strange habits and a tendency to keep mountaineers waiting).

High on a rocky path approximately halfway up the

Twelve, Diek Wustapha stopped dead before a rock wall and listened. Moments before, he'd emerged from the clouds like an apparition, stepping down through thin air as if an invisible staircase existed to serve the purpose. The children had followed in a straight, orderly line, their eyes focused on some distant preoccupation.

And, still, Diek listened.

A number of the smaller children, thoroughly hypnotized by a tune that now existed only in their heads, cannoned into him. He pushed them back, drew in a breath and raised his arms. The voice that came forth was not his own.

Eliumariss Toomathane. Rastarinimpetus Kadant!

For a time, nothing happened. Diek just stood, motionless before the rock-face, watching some far-off lightshow with his borrowed eyes. He took a few tentative steps, then strode right through the barrier as though it had never existed. One by one, the children followed him beyond the illusion and down, down into the darkness.

Far below . . .

Gordo's decision to go *around* the base of the Twelve had turned out to be a very unfortunate one in terms of progress. This series of hindrances had begun with a chance meeting between the party and a group of nomads who'd set up camp in the gargantuan mountain's lower foothills. The nomads mixed warm hospitality with a seemingly endless supply of ale and, consequently, the group had been in their company for the best part of a day. Now, following some friendly nomad advice about several dangerous creatures lurking on the Twelve's eastern base, they'd elected to go *over* the mountain instead. To do this successfully, Tambor had reasoned, they needed to start from the well-worn path which they'd been on the day before, and that meant starting the whole journey from scratch. During these difficult hours, much of their journey was spent in silence (or at least the sort of silence that's regularly interrupted by muffled curses).

A glimmer on the horizon signalled that thunder was lurking and a bitter wind whistled down the path, making all necessary progress as difficult as possible. Unlike many of Illmoor's treacherous regions, the Twelve was allotted no specific deity to whom prayers of safe passage could be directed. This classified it as one of the 'limbo lands', godless areas which fell under the power of any god who happened to pass through. Judging by the weather it was Token, god of sudden showers. Token was a deity with very few actual followers, although every year the few he had would gather on the summit of the Twelve to witness an event they referred to as 'The Great Drenching'.

'I don't suppose either of you carry a readable map of the area?' Tambor said, his teeth chattering in the wind.

Groan and Gordo stared blankly at each other. Then

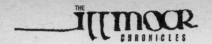
they cast a glance in every direction, hopeful for some sign of a settlement that wouldn't involve conquering the mountain.

'I take it that's a no, then?' the old man continued.

'Oh, look at this,' Gordo replied. 'It's not enough that we've landed up with a sorcerer with no spell-book, now he's whinging into the bargain.'

Tambor averted his eyes. He had a rolled-up carpet under one arm, which he'd collected from his lodgings in Laker Street. It was a magic carpet, he'd assured them, but one that definitely wouldn't support a man of Groan's size and stature. He had just been preparing to take off, when he'd remembered his missing spell-book and the not insubstantial conjuration that was required to start the thing.

Gordo spat at the grass and fiddled with a strap beneath his helmet.

Eventually it became unhooked.

'We should go back,' he said. 'I saw something last night that I didn't much like the look of. I think there was a magic—'

'Damn magic,' said Groan. 'An' damn the city. 'S never done us no favours.'

'I just thought maybe we could have a look . . .'

'You're goin' soft, Gordo Goldeaxe.'

'I am not!' the dwarf protested, taking instant offence at the full use of his name. 'But we don't know where we're going! You might walk the land, Groan Teethgrit, but some of us have homes and families that love and care for a dwarf ... who brings home gold for the village.'

He dropped his battleaxe, slumped on to a rotting tree stump and began beating himself over the head with the dangling chinstrap of his helmet.

'I'm fed up with this travelling lark,' he said. 'I wish I'd stayed in the village with Uncle Grimson.'

'There might be a village in the foothills,' said Tambor. Groan sniffed and peered up at the Twelve.

A flash of lightning lit up the sky.

'There'd better be,' said Gordo, snatching up his battleaxe.

Geographical interlude ...

Examine Illmoor: a great wedge-shaped chunk of land surrounded by ocean.

Two tiny circles indicating two minute towns that bookend the wider half of the land and an inky blob indicating a sprawling capital that sits in the crevice at its southernmost point.

The capital? Dullitch, home to a wider assortment of crooks, vagabonds and mixed-species mugging squads than any single ruler can comfortably handle. A polluted, crime-ridden flea-pit of eccentricity, where man walks arm-in-arm with dwarf, troll walks arm-in-arm with man and dwarf walks arm-in-arm with troll (figuratively speaking). Admittedly, in the case of the

last this is more of a dusty, fist-hurling ball, complete with occasional shouts of 'great stone git!', and generally ends with a dwarf called Flatfoot really living up to his name.

The towns? Legrash and Spittle. Two communities; each competitive and self-serving and each reluctant for the other to prosper. The prestigious Legrash, famed for its Pirates Guild, and the towering Spittle, renowned for a network of spies so paranoid that they spend most of their time watching each other. Thankfully, the two are separated by many different kinds of landscape: dense woodland, vast mountain regions and meadows that stretch on (seemingly) for ever.

But the trio of pinpricks carefully negotiating the Twelve weren't too hot on geography (Groan suspected it had something to do with keeping fit) and, unlike Diek, they didn't have the advantage of being aided by magic.

They were a quarter of the way up the mountain, when Groan suddenly stopped them dead in their tracks.

'Don't like it 'ere,' said Groan. 'It's too quiet. I reckon they're all waitin' in the trees to jump out on us.'

'Who?'

'Them.'

Groan sniffed. As far as he was concerned 'us' was whoever he was with and 'them' was anybody else.

Gordo swung his battleaxe experimentally.

An arrow landed in the grass beside the path. Upright.

''S an arrow,' announced Groan, in case anyone had missed it.

No one moved. A few seconds passed without incident. Somewhere off among the trees, a shadow shifted. Tambor took this as his cue to make a definite exit and dived into a convenient bush at the side of the path. Three more arrows rained down upon the group.

'I'd just like to point out,' whispered Tambor, from behind his bush, 'that I think you can take this bravery thing a bit too far.'

'I've got nothing to worry about,' said Gordo, out of the corner of his mouth. 'Small target.'

Tambor muttered something under his breath and tried to dig a hole beneath the bush by scooping out mounds of dirt with his hands.

'Coward,' said Groan.

Gordo grimaced. Four arrows was fair indication of trouble.

'What is it, d'you think?' he asked, staring at the barbarian hopefully. 'Trolls? Orcs?'

A fifth arrow landed just beyond Tambor's bush and the sorcerer yelped.

Groan shook his head.

'Too 'igh for orcs,' he said. 'Too low fer trolls.'

'Great,' whispered Tambor. 'Now we know who's definitely *not* attacking us. Any chance of a guess in the opposite direction? Only, I'd like to know who to curse when I'm picking an arrowhead out of my aaaarrhh—'

The sorcerer leapt out of his bush, danced around in circles for a few seconds and then dived back in.

'What was that?' asked Gordo.

Tambor coughed. 'Hedgehog,' he snapped. 'Find somewhere to hide, will you?'

'It's OK,' said Gordo. 'I think they might've gone.'

'Don't be ridiculous!' said Tambor. 'You don't fire five arrows at someone and then just walk away.'

Groan shrugged.

'P'raps it's a greetin',' he said.

'Very friendly,' said Tambor. 'Don't fancy visiting *their* village.'

The rain intensified, turning from thin drizzle into a heavy shower.

Tambor sneezed and flicked away some of the rainwater dripping from the brim of his hat. He was just about to start complaining when the sixth arrow arrived.

Jimmy Quickstint galloped on down the road. It was nice of the duke to lend him this wonderful horse, he thought. It was far better than the resentful brute he'd been given as a scout. Apparently it had once belonged to Sir Rolf the Bruce, a knight made famous by his instinct for desertion. Jimmy patted it affectionately in the hope that it would slow down. He wondered if it was used to untrained riders. The horse itself didn't wonder about anything. It was glad of the company.

Mountains loomed ahead. Jimmy tried to think clearly.

Presuming the two mercenaries were still with his granddad, they would probably have headed for Legrash. He looked up at the mountains and decided that no fool would attempt to climb something they could go around. After a lengthy struggle, he managed to point the horse towards a patch of forest around the base of the Twelve. Then he reached down and slapped it on the flank, which turned out to be a big mistake.

'You said orcs wouldn't be this far up!' Tambor screamed. He was sprinting up and down the path with remarkable speed for a man of more than eighty years. A short distance away Groan was slamming heads together, six at a time in some cases.

'Maybe these ones are ambitious,' shouted Gordo, swinging his battleaxe around a widening circle of greenskins. 'You know, the intellectual type.'

'Intellectual orcs?' yelled Tambor. 'Well that's just terrific, isn't it?' He ducked down as a sabre whistled past.

A screech echoed from above and a Garji-rider swooped low over the mountainside. Groan took one look up at the sky and dashed off into the woods at the side of the road.

'Where are you going?' screamed Tambor.

'Get a tree to fro' at 'em,' the barbarian shouted back.

Gordo had made a very important decision and promised the dwarf gods that, should he escape now, he

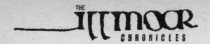
would never leave his village again. Divine intervention came in the form of a large pebble, which he tripped on, narrowly avoiding a sabre hurled by one of the greenskins. Instead, it bit into the shoulder of another. Lucky, Gordo thought to himself, but I'd have preferred a lightning bolt or something.

Groan came thundering out of the woods, a small tree balanced on one shoulder. He stopped running, reached back and pitched it at the winged monstrosity. It missed.

'Where are you going now?' screamed Tambor, who was perched on the lowest branch of a nearby oak.

'Get annuva one,' shouted Groan.

'We haven't got time!' yelled Gordo, above the fray. 'Besides, you'd probably miss again.'

Groan scowled.

'Never missed anyfin' twice,' he said. Never hit anyfin' twice, he thought.

Tambor had experienced a sudden flash of inspiration. Maybe he could get the carpet working if he remembered exactly the right words. He felt around beside him but his fingers just found bark. He thought: the carpet's still in the bush. He peered over at Gordo, who was struggling against a greenskin waving what looked like a shovel.

'Hey, Gordo! Could you pass me my carpet?'

The dwarf's reply was lost on the wind, which was probably for the best.

*

'Come back!' Jimmy shouted, waving his arms frantically as the horse galloped back towards Dullitch. 'Please! I need . . . oh no, somebody help!'

He stood and watched as the knight's steed became a speck on the horizon. Then he looked round at the forest, sat down cross-legged and began to sob.

The battleaxe flew through the air and buried itself in the stomach of the Garji, whose rider screamed and dived off. Tambor shrieked, Gordo smiled and even Groan looked momentarily taken aback. The elation didn't last for long. A cold scream echoed round the mountain as a second group of greenskins poured into the clearing, scrambling over one another in an attempt to draw first blood.

Gordo's battleaxe danced in a complicated arc around him, opening gashes and lopping off limbs, while Groan was employing half a branch to swat away the brave few who dared approach him. However, their numbers were increasing, and Tambor fancied that he could make out a second line of orcs in the shadows around the clearing. Even with Groan as a deterrent, he had to admit the situation didn't look good.

Fifteen

What Jimmy had taken to be a forest was unexpectedly turning out to be more of a jungle.

Incredible, he thought. Outside it's freezing cold and in here it's like the oven of the gods. It would be fair to say that he was not enjoying the beauty of the wild. He didn't know what was worse, losing the royal horse or losing all the money intended to lure the mercenaries back. Time was probably running out for the children of Dullitch and here he was, stranded in some dense wilderness, without any hope of ever finding the mercenaries and no money to pay them even if he did! The whole day had been one big disaster. Come to think about it, his whole *life* was one big disaster.

He coughed and swatted away a few mosquitoes.

There were trees in every direction. He imagined a pair of eyes beneath every twig, hissing and biting at anything that didn't qualify as a member of the same species which, in a jungle of this size, amounted to just about everything. A crescendo of unpleasant sounds was building in the distance, as a pack of undiscovered terrors hunted down some poor primate with one leg and a screech like a cat in a combine-harvester. He expected an explosion of jagged claws and needle-sharp teeth at any moment. A small, featherless monstrosity of unknown origin squawked a hideous cacophony from a nearby tree. I'm lost, he thought. That's the second time I've been past that tree with the red arrow scrawled on it.

He tripped over a tree root, then gave it a vengeful kick. A branch that lay horizontally across the path opened half an eye and slithered away behind a tree-stump. Jimmy shivered; he'd had a dreadful fear of snakes ever since his grandfather had told him that his favourite uncle had been strangled by a feather boa.

The recollection didn't do much to calm his nerves; the quicker he got out of this place, the better.

Jimmy was, in fact, struggling through the Carafat jungles, north of Dullitch, which played host to some of the oldest (and indeed most terrible) tribes in Illmoor. The Carif Backslashers, Gib's Minions, the winged hordes of Yud the Acolyte, Trumnf Caew's Marauders –

they all have a stake here. Wander into this territory by accident, and you won't last five minutes.

Not neglecting to mention the spear traps triggered by a spit in the wrong direction, the death mazes where twisted minds painted misleading arrows on the walls using their own blood, and freak log slides that could roll you flatter than a pancake. In Carafat, the only thing more dangerous than standing still was moving.

Jimmy had heard mention of a handful of notorious expeditions, most successful of which had been one led by a man called Passion. After months of catastrophic torture at the hands of a mysterious heathen death-squad, Passion had returned with some insightful advice to all would-be travellers. Unfortunately, it was stapled to his head and written in hieroglyphs, and no one knew a really good medium so they never found out what it was.

Something large with no shortage of feathers flew in Jimmy's face, and he reached up and smacked it aside. It hit a sweating palm and spent the next few seconds hobbling around on the floor complaining about it. Jimmy stepped away from the creature and took a good look. It wasn't surprising Dullitch didn't have an aviary. There really wasn't much to like about birds, he decided. Especially birds of prey. Where was the connection, for goodness sake? He tried to think of a sacred psalm with the word 'vulture' in it.

A vine swung loose from a nearby tree and dangled

provocatively in front of him. I'm not falling for *that* one, he thought.

The path he was following ended rather abruptly at a rock-face. It looked false. Jimmy cocked his head and closed one eye, a habit of his which kicked in whenever he had to size up a situation mentally. There was definitely the outline of a door there, a sort of rectangle etched into the stone. He pushed gently, then put all his weight against it to give him proper leverage. There was a tiny creak, another screech and an unrelated rumble in the distance; apart from that, nothing happened. He swore under his breath, stepped back and gave the slab an experimental kick.

Several tons of rock slid away, revealing a small portal and a set of dusty stairs leading down into the darkness.

Far, far below, deep inside the heart of the Twelve, Diek Wustapha stood atop a rock in a draughty chasm. Below him, a sea of tiny faces stared upwards, eyes glazed, captivated by the magic which swirled around the focus of their affection. The magic was visible now, a frenzied purple cloud glittering liberally with frozen stars.

Shaken from his reverie only to accede to the wishes of the voice, Diek Wustapha raised the flute to his lips and began to play.

A hum went up from his young audience, resonating around the chasm like a ball dropped into a drum.

All the life I need is here, Diek, came the terrible tones. *On this, I can exist for centuries. You have done well.*

$\mathcal{S}ixteen$

It had taken fifteen orc warriors to drag Groan to the ground and a further three to snare him in irons. Gordo had put up a fair fight himself, eventually overcome by four heavy greenskin scouts. Tambor came a little easier; in fact, he'd surrendered even before the orcs had noticed him.

A miniature fanfare proceeded. It wasn't much of one (comprising purely of drum beats), but apparently the orcs were used to it. A few of them wore the embarrassed expression familiar to members of any organization that employs ceremonial song as it troops its colours.

The tribe chieftain arrived to look over his prisoners.

He was a grotty little orc, stout of gut and long of tooth, with enough souvenirs dangling from around his neck to intimate that he ran a very successful outfit.

He prodded Groan in the arm, spat at Tambor and gave Gordo a sharp kick in the ribs. Then he snatched up the dwarf's battleaxe and waved his arm in the direction of the wood. A succession of mumbles died away and the tribe began to move.

'Psst,' said Tambor. His arms were chained to a sort of log pulley-system without the log. 'Psst!'

Groan continued to walk with his head down. The rest of his body was constricted by chains.

'Oi!'

The barbarian glanced over at Tambor.

'Yeah?' he said.

'Do you think you could break your chains?'

'Dunno.'

'Why don't you try, then?'

'Try what?'

Tambor rolled his eyes. He had a feeling he could spend the rest of his life having this conversation.

'Why don't you try to break them?'

'What with?'

'Forget I mentioned it.'

Tambor yelped. The chains were beginning to grind on his hands. He hurried to catch up with his gaoler.

Gordo was having a slightly easier time of it. Apparently none of the orcs had been prepared to walk along bending over, so they'd made some kind of platform for him to stand on.

Tambor struggled against his chains and got a sharp slap in the face for his efforts. He waited until his head had stopped spinning, then turned and gave Gordo a half-smile.

'I expect you've been orc-napped a few times, eh?' he said. 'Incidentally, do you know the one about the mongoose and—'

'Shut it, coward.'

'Well, that's nice, isn't it?' said Tambor. 'Considering I'm about to save us all from certain death.'

Gordo turned a beady eye on the sorcerer. Even Groan listened in.

'I think,' said Tambor, twitching to relieve an itch in his beard, 'that I may be able to remember a very good offensive spell.'

Groan sniffed. He hated magic.

'What's that?' said Gordo suspiciously.

'It's called "Tower of Screaming Doom",' said Tambor. 'If I can do it right, a spinning column twenty feet tall should appear in the air and wipe out anyone standing.'

'Well, can you do it or not?' said Gordo, excitedly.

'I think so.'

Groan heard the sorcerer mumble something in a foreign tongue.

'When I say "now",' Tambor whispered, 'I want you both to dive for the ground.'

The mercenaries murmured in agreement.

'NOW!'

Tambor muttered an incantation and dived theatrically to the ground as a spinning column of flame winked into existence above him. It soared high over the heads of the tallest orcs but no one paid very much attention because, apart from the fact that they were all surprised by the erratic behaviour of their captive, the spinning column was approximately five inches high.

Groan used the momentary confusion to break through his chains. Or, rather, he chose that moment to break through his chains. Momentary confusions tended to leave Groan momentarily confused. Orcs flew in all directions.

Gordo leaped from his platform and cannoned into Tambor's captor. The 'Tower of Screaming Doom' devastated a nearby beehive before fizzling out.

Jimmy Quickstint peered into the shadowy darkness lurking just beyond the first few steps. The way he saw it, there were two choices. He could either turn back, run home to Dullitch and face the wrath of Duke Modeset, or he could go ahead and chance that the portal would stay open, in case he decided to run back after all. Simple, really.

He reached out a tentative foot and brought it down on the top step. Nothing happened. Then he stepped inside. A flock of birds erupted from the treetops behind and he spun around, breathing heavily. Nothing happened.

Jimmy swallowed and offered a silent prayer to the god of ignorant thieves, hoping that there was one. Then he closed his eyes, clenched his fists and descended the first three steps. Nothing happened. Thank the lords for that, he thought, leaning against the inner wall. Perhaps there really was a god looking out for him, after all.

Something in the Stygian gloom below made a 'crraaawwl' noise. Jimmy froze with fear. The stone slab rolled back into place and locked with a decisive click.

'That was a close one,' said Tambor, staring around the clearing with a satisfied smile. 'Good thing I know my business.'

The battle in the woods was over. It had drawn to a swift conclusion when Groan had happened upon the tactic of using one orc to hit another. He brushed a mouldy leaf off his shoulder and flexed.

'Good fight,' he said, grinning.

'Yep,' said Tambor. 'Don't mess with magic, that's what I say.'

'Magic?' exclaimed Gordo, leaning on his battleaxe. 'You didn't *do* anything!'

Tambor looked amazed.

'What about the Tower of Screaming Doom!' he shouted.

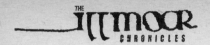

'What about it?'

'Didn't you see it?'

'No.'

'It flew around for ages.'

'I saw it,' said Groan. 'Smacked it over that way.'

He pointed over at a twisted oak-tree, where half a beehive was smouldering.

'Ingrates!' said Tambor, shaking his fists. 'That was earth-magic at work, that was! Will somebody get me out of these chains!'

Illmoor is, at its heart, a land rooted in magic. As such, it has its fair share of supernatural beings and spiritual entities. It also has a number of gods, one for just about anything you would want to imagine, including a few for things you wouldn't want to imagine.

Perhaps the strangest of these is Dirgo, god of Disturbing Sounds. Doomed to sufferance eternal, he frequents hidden temples and secret passageways, seeking would-be heroes for his peculiar brand of terror.

From his rooms in the palace of Harkon, home of the gods, he looked down on Jimmy Quickstint, breath held, creeping down a flight of steps deep inside the Twelve. He flicked through his book of 'Vocal Species' and turned to the section headed 'Amphibious Exhalations'.

'Croaaarrrrkk!'

Jimmy took half a step back, slipped and tumbled

head-over-heels down the staircase. He landed at the bottom in an awkward heap.

When a few seconds had passed without anything biting a chunk from his ankle, he forced himself up on to his elbows and began to look around.

Spent torches hung from ancient braziers on the walls. From what he could make out, he was on a landing of some kind. There was a cell in the far wall. It had one occupant.

'What a spot of luck,' the man said, stretching out a hand between the bars of his prison. 'Thought we were goners, we did.'

Jimmy boggled at him.

'Who are you?' he said.

'I'm Stump, and this here is Mick. We're prisoners, as you've probably guessed.'

Jimmy strained to look inside the cage. He couldn't see anything.

'Is there somebody else in there with you?' he asked.

Stump peered around behind him.

'Nah,' he said. 'It's just me and Mick.' A flake of dust fell out of his beard. 'Doubt if there'd be room in here for three of us,' he added.

'How long have you been in there?'

'A while, I reckon. Mick was here already.'

'Who locked you up?'

'Oh, nobody *locked* us up. These caves are old, really old, and the tribes that used to lurk hereabouts had a

habit of diggin' out long tunnels and plungin' pits all over the surface above. I fell through like a good'un. Serves me right for not lookin' where I was goin. Reckon you could get us out?'

Jimmy nodded. 'No problem, there isn't a lock in the land I can't break.'

Gordo wiped some green slime from the head of his battleaxe. The temperature was dropping rapidly and a thin mist had begun to coil among the trees. The forest was becoming darker and gloomier by the minute.

'See all the crushed twigs?' said Gordo. 'I reckon this place is crawling with orcs, and we certainly don't want any more surprises.'

Groan suddenly snatched hold of Tambor and flung him into the lower branches of the nearest tree.

'What was *that* for?' snapped the sorcerer. 'Have you any idea how old I am?'

'Climb up, tell us what you see.'

'What, all the way to the top?'

'Yeah.'

'You should be careful,' Gordo whispered, when Tambor was three-quarters of the way to the top. 'He is getting on, you know.'

'I've bin finkin' 'bout that,' said Groan. 'Did you see the way he jumped for that bush out on the road?'

'So?' Gordo said, brows furrowed. He didn't like it when the barbarian started to think for himself.

'I reckon there's somefin' goin' on there,' said Groan suspiciously. 'I don't reckon he's as old as he makes out.'

'But he's got to be! I mean, I remember he was quite famous when I first came to Dullitch, way back. Tambor Forestall! Everyone knew about Tambor Forestall back then. I'm sure of it. Tambor Forestall and the Seven Dragons, Tambor Forestall and the Trolls of Epsworth Creek, Tambor Forestall and, and . . .'

'. . . and the Tower of Screamin' Doom?' ventured Groan. He smiled; sarcasm was a new experience for him.

Tambor was slowly descending from the top of the tree. He slipped on one of the lower branches and landed on the forest floor with a crash.

'Well,' he said eventually, 'there's good news and there's bad news. Which do you want first?'

Gordo shrugged. 'Either.'

'Well,' Tambor continued, getting to his feet. 'The good news is, we've lost the orcs. The bad news is, we have to go back the way we came.'

'Why?'

'There's a giant chopping wood about two clearings ahead of us.'

'A giant?'

'Yes. G-i-a-n-t. Giant. He's twice the size of Groan.' The old sorcerer shook his head. 'I suppose he might be friendly, but I doubt it. Either way, we can't take the risk.'

'We won't then,' Groan muttered. 'I'll just knock 'im out.'

'What?' Tambor looked down at Gordo. 'Did you hear that? He's out of his stupid mind. That's a giant, for crying out loud. He'll get us all killed!'

The dwarf shrugged. 'Stay here if you like,' he said, unclasping his battleaxe. 'I doubt this'll take long.'

'Hey!' Tambor called after them. 'Is there any chance of nipping back to fetch my carpet?'

Deep inside the Twelve there was a barely audible 'clink' and the prison door swung open.

'That's incredible!' said Stump. 'We're impressed.'

Jimmy was about to point out that he couldn't actually see anybody else in the cell, when the thought was postponed by a queue-jumper.

'You haven't seen anything unusual since you've been up here, have you?' he asked.

Stump squinted back at the cage.

'Like what?'

'Well, like an eight-foot barbarian, an old sorcerer and a dwarf.'

'Nope, sorry,' he said, smiling. 'Haven't seen anyone like that. Don't know about Mick, he was already down here when I arrived. He might've seen somethin'. You can ask him yourself.'

Jimmy smiled sympathetically.

'Insanity's a terrible thing,' he muttered.

'What's that?'

'Er . . . I said it must've been horrible to be locked up down here all that time.'

'Oh, not really,' said Stump, shaking his head. 'We kept ourselves busy, you know how it is.' He scratched a stubbly upper lip. 'The first few days were the worst, gettin' to know each other, like. We had a couple of cross words *then*. Mick's no good at I-spy,' he added, winking conspiratorially.

'Fine,' said Jimmy.

'Plus,' Stump continued, unabashed, 'you wouldn't believe how many people just walk right by, don't even lift a finger when they hear a bloke in distress; ain't that right, Mick? Flamin' scoutmasters.'

Jimmy frowned. 'Scoutmasters?'

'Yeah,' said Stump reasonably. 'At any rate, he looked like a scoutmaster. He had a lot of kids with him, didn't he, Mick?'

Back in Dullitch, the city's fragile morale was beginning to crack.

'I'm sorry, the *what*?' Modeset asked, leaning across his desk and cupping a hand to his ear.

'The, er, the Dullitch Society for the Successful Location and Safe Return of Missing Children, milord.'

'And they're demanding my abdication?'

'Yes, milord.'

'Nonsense! I've never even heard of them. In fact, I'd

be surprised if they existed before lunch.'

Pegrand smiled nervously. 'They say they've been going twenty years, milord. You know, on the off-chance.'

'Ah yes, like the Association for Making Friends with the People of Phlegm Before They Invade Us Next Tuesday? Or even, what was it, the Long Established League Against the Early Closing of the Rotting Ferret on a Friday Night? Ha! They must think I was born upside down in a haystack. Tell them to drop dead.'

'Yes, milord.'

'But not in those words, of course.'

''Course not, milord.' Pegrand shuffled some documents and hurried out. He returned a few moments later with a different set. 'They did have this, though.'

Modeset sighed and rubbed his eyelids.

'What is it?'

'Er, well, it's a petition demanding answers, milord.'

'Is it signed?'

'Yes, milord.'

'Just the one page?'

'Er, yes, milord. Oh, no, tell a lie, there's two. Unless this one's part . . . oh right, three. Oh, no, four . . . and the two I've just dropped.'

'GIVE IT TO ME!'

Modeset reached up, snatched the sheaf of documents and threw them straight into the bin.

'Now go and find Quaris Sands!' he snapped. 'We need a workable speech by the morning and I'm damn sure I'm not going to be the one writing it.'

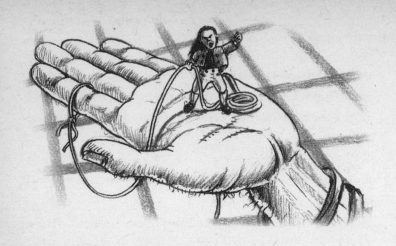

Seventeen

Jimmy was trying to get a grip on his excitement.

'Let me get this straight,' he said. 'You saw a stranger leading a large group of children through here?'

'Yeah, like I said.' Stump yawned. 'There's a grate in the back of the cell, you see. I saw 'em all filing past in the next tunnel, so I shouted for help. Funny thing was, they didn't even hear me! It was like they were all hypnotized or somethin'. Totally zonked. Are you all right? You look like you've seen a ghost.'

Jimmy swallowed, swallowed and swallowed again.

'Please listen to me very carefully,' he began, his hands shaking violently as he spoke. 'My name is Jimmy Quickstint, I come from Dullitch. That scoutmaster is some kind of evil enchanter. He *stole* those children from Dullitch and I need to get them back before, well, before he decides to do something unspeakable to them.'

'That's awful!' Stump gasped. 'Hang on though, wait a minute; are you telling me they've sent you out on your own to stop this fella?'

'No, not exactly. I was supposed to find these mercenaries who're travelling with my granddad – he's an ex-sorcerer, by the way – and oh, it's all too complicated to explain now! Listen, do you think there's any way we can get through this wall?'

Stump peered into his cell for what seemed like a long time.

'No,' he said eventually, turning back. 'But you shouldn't need to. The Twelve's full of these tunnels; one big network from the outside in; junctions all over the place. You just have to follow *this* tunnel through; no doubts it'll link up to the others somewhere along the line. Maybe Mick would know, he's lived down here for years.'

This time, Jimmy just couldn't let the question go unspoken.

'Is Mick a ghost?' he asked tentatively.

Stump frowned at him.

'Mick doesn't know whether to be insulted or not by that remark.'

'Oh, sorry. Tell him I apologize.'

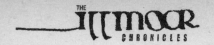

'Look,' said Stump, suddenly straightening up. 'I ain't no mediator; tell him yourself.'

'I CAN'T SEE HIM!' shouted Jimmy. He shoved the prisoner aside, marched into the cell and walked twice around it. Then he got down on his hands and knees to crawl under a sloping wall in the rear of the room. Stump watched with a detached amusement.

'What are you up to?' he asked.

'I'm just trying to prove to myself,' said Jimmy, prodding a leg into parts the rest of him couldn't reach, 'that I'm not going crazy. There is no Mick.'

'Did you hear that, Mick? He says you don't exist.'

The thief struggled to his feet and shook his head. Of all the prisoners in all the cells, in all the lands, he thought, why did I have to get this lunatic?

Then he saw Mick waving at him.

Standing on the prisoner's palm was a man two inches tall. He was wearing britches and a jerkin. He had a tiny eye-patch over one eye. Jimmy gaped at him.

'See?' said Stump, excitedly. 'That's Mick, that is.'

'Flimder,' said Mick.

'What is he?' Jimmy asked, fascinated.

'Mick's a mite, says he's the bastard son of Tim Index. He don't say much, but I think we understand each other on a kind of spiritual level. He might be telepathic.'

The little man produced a miniature rope and looped

the end over Stump's forefinger. Then he started to abseil down the prisoner's hand.

'Look at him,' said Stump cheerfully. 'He's always tryin' to get away.'

Jimmy watched as he flicked his wrist and caught the mite back in the palm of his hand.

'He's a real one for escaping, is Mick.'

'But that's ridiculous! He could've walked between the bars at any time.'

'Eh?'

Jimmy shook his head in disbelief.

'You said,' he began, trying to speak in plain language in case Stump was having problems in that department, 'that he was already here when you arrived. Why didn't he just leave?'

'I think he'd made himself at home, to be honest. He had a nice little house built out of an old tinderbox.'

'What happened to that?' said Jimmy, looking around again.

'I landed on it.'

'Flimder,' said Mick, shaking a minuscule fist at the prisoner.

'You know something, Stump?'

'What's that?'

'I don't think Mick likes you very much.'

Jimmy slumped down on to the dusty stone and wiped some sweat from his forehead with the back of his hand.

'So,' he said. 'We know the children are down here

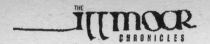

somewhere. If we find them, that leaves me to fight the enchanter. Great, just great. I wonder where Granddad is?'

Groan Teethgrit was experiencing a situation which, to his mind, simply didn't add up. Usually when he threw punches people fell; most times they just fell over and, occasionally, they fell thousands of feet. They never just stood there looking at him. Groan felt as if he was punching a cushion.

The giant just stood, motionless, and continued to glare.

'C'mon then,' Groan managed, after the third blow had failed to garner a reaction. 'I'm not touchin' sword, this is fightin' ol' style, han' to han'. Lesee what you got.'

The giant reeled back and gave him a slap. Groan sailed backwards, hitting a young Coomba tree so hard that he actually heard the roots splitting as he lost consciousness.

The giant stepped amidst the rubble and reached down to pick up the comatose barbarian. Unexpectedly, he got a battleaxe buried in his back. It felt like a wasp sting.

Gordo yanked as hard as he could but the axe simply wouldn't cut loose. He put one foot on the giant's back for leverage and found himself on the receiving end of a slap from a hand of lily-pad proportions. The giant didn't see where Gordo landed, but he *did* see, out of the corner of his eye, an old man running towards him, frantically waving a broken branch. He stretched out a fist and there was a dull thud. The branch fell to the floor.

The giant yawned, removed the axe from his back and hung it on a belt hook. Then he slung Tambor over one shoulder, snatched hold of Groan's boots and began dragging the barbarian back through the forest. On the way, he collected Gordo Goldeaxe, who'd landed upside down in a briar patch.

In the far distance, a coil of smoke headed skyward. The giant smiled. He always lit a succession of small fires whenever he went out to chop wood. They marked the path back to the entrance of his cave in the mountainside. He headed towards it with his new prisoners, feeling that on the whole life couldn't get much better.

Eighteen

Stump had secreted Mick about his person. Jimmy didn't like to ask where.

This is ridiculous, he thought. Even if I do find out where the foreigner took them, how am I ever going to sneak hundreds of children out of a mountain without him noticing?

'Look,' he said eventually, employing what he hoped was a friendly smile. 'I've got to start looking. Can you help me?'

'No.'

Jimmy boggled at him.

'No? You won't help me rescue kidnapped children?'

'The thing is,' Stump continued, 'it feels like I've been

down here for ages and I wanna go back and see my family, you know how it is. Beryl, that's my wife, she's probably remarried, thinkin' I'm a goner.'

'Oh, right,' said Jimmy. 'You'd better get back to her, then.'

'Yeah, well, you know how it is. Sorry about that; good luck and all.'

'Thanks. I think.'

Jimmy nodded, got to his feet and marched off towards the lower staircase.

'No hard feelings,' Stump called after him. 'I'm sure you*aaaahhh* . . . Mick! Stop bitin' me nipple!'

'Tambor?'

Eyelids flickered. A light in the darkness; small, indistinct. It hovered around at the edge of the sorcerer's field of vision. Then, slowly, shapes began to swim into focus. He saw a lot of faces, no, correction; he saw a lot of *face* . . .

'You're all right, then?' said Gordo.

'Let's not jump to any conclusions.'

'I thought you might be dead.'

Tambor stared blearily around the room. It seemed to be a cell of some kind. He noted the half-rusted chains and manacles that hung from every wall. A tiny grille offered one of only two light sources, the other being a rather pathetic candle, half-melted, on a shelf above Gordo's head. There were also some

half-rotted torches stacked in one corner.

The dwarf was kneeling beside him. Blood leaked
from a cut on his forehead and his clothes were in
tatters. Despite all this, he seemed as companionable as
ever. Groan was lying flat out like a felled oak. He
twitched every few seconds. Gordo hadn't seen a twitch
like that since his father had sworn off alcohol.

The sorcerer moaned. A dull throb which had started
in the base of his spine was gradually working its way
north, planning a terrible assault on his neck and
shoulders.

'What happened?' he said.

'Well, I don't know what happened to *you*, but we've
taken a right old belting. Groan got KO'd by the giant,
and I tried to help but he knocked me flying. Then I
think he must have dragged us up to his cave. Groan
was spark out, but I came round pretty quick.' He
grinned with masculine pride. 'I'm tougher than I look.'

'You'd have to be. So, in fact, we're *inside* a cell *inside*
the giant's cave *inside* the mountain. Sound right?'

'Yep, that's the way of it.'

'I don't understand; why would he keep us here?'

'Who knows? Maybe he'll ransom us.'

Tambor nodded, and had a good go at a positively
wretched expression. As his vision improved, so the
scene around him was becoming progressively worse.
When things were bad they were bad; you didn't want
details.

For example, he hadn't seen the snake before. It slithered from a hole in the wall and wriggled into a crevice beneath the stone staircase. A number of indescribable obscenities crawled, on a wide ratio of legs, across the cell floor. Tambor closed his eyes and pretended he was somewhere sunny.

There was a commotion outside, the cell door flew open and three plates were thrown in, landing face down on the stone. The door closed again.

Tambor managed to fight off a few of the milder monstrosities to gain possession of something that looked like a distant relation of the dumpling.

He bit hard, closed his eyes and swallowed.

'I expect he's fattening us up,' he told Gordo. 'Well, fattening one of us up. He might want to starve you.'

'He'd better not,' snapped the dwarf. 'Before we got into this mess, I hadn't missed a single meal in thirty years.'

'Figures,' said Tambor.

He struggled to his feet and kicked some dust over a dubious shadow in the corner. When it didn't slink back or make a dive for his leg, he gave it a tentative tap with the toe of his boot. It turned out to be an old rag. He subjected it to a malicious stare, and then kicked some more dust over it.

'Well, that's us done for, then,' he said. Gordo gazed up at him, his face radiating surprise.

'Really?' he said. 'I was sure you'd think of something.

You sorcerers always struck me as the intelligent sort, 'specially when it comes to escape and the like.'

'Oh, we are, generally speaking,' said Tambor. 'It's just that, well, being a sorcerer with a bad memory and no spell-book doesn't really prepare you for a prison break, if you know what I mean.'

'Mmm. I see your point,' said Gordo. 'So, that's it. We're doomed.'

'So it would appear.'

They sat sharing the embarrassed silence for a while, before Gordo jumped to his feet.

'I've got an idea,' he said.

Tambor brightened considerably. For the last few minutes he'd been suffering under the misapprehension that the dwarf had been bitten by one of the cell's poisonous co-habitants. He'd seen ideas dawn on people before, but never like that. Gordo gave the term 'stroke of genius' a literal meaning.

'Why don't we turn out our pockets and see if we've got anything that might get us out?' he said.

'Fine,' said Tambor. 'I've got a mousetrap and a piece of cheese. How about you?'

'Er, oh . . . I don't have anything. Sorry.'

'Good plan, though.'

'Thanks,' said Gordo.

'I'm going to sleep now. Wake me up if anything dramatic happens.'

*

Jimmy had been wandering along the same dank tunnel for what seemed like hours. He looked at the walls either side of him, wondering if it was one of those deceptive tunnels, where it appeared as if you were getting somewhere when you were actually just walking around in a circle.

It was gloomy too; secret tunnels and passageways beneath a mountain should surely be covered in symbols or runes or *something*. Not like this one, all brown and sewery. He reached out and touched a wall which felt pretty much the same as the walls back home.

Jimmy was just wondering whether he should check for hidden doors or concealed levers when he heard footsteps approaching. He panicked and ran along the passage a little way, his head throbbing as he searched for somewhere to hide. There was nowhere. How could you hide in a place like this? He realized that the only way to survive would probably be to surprise whoever it was and the only way he could do that would be to lie down on the floor and suddenly leap up, before he was trodden on. Things didn't go according to plan.

'Ahh! My nose—'

'Sorry, mate.'

Jimmy looked up and could just about make out a grubby countenance staring down at him.

'Stump?' he managed. 'I thought you'd gone.'

'Couldn't get past the rock-door,' said the prisoner, looking around the tunnel with a grim smile.

'No, I tried getting back out that way when I first came in,' said Jimmy.

'Sick and tired of this place.'

'I'm not surprised. Good of you to come back, anyway. Even though you didn't have any option.'

'Exactly,' said Stump. 'So, how are you gettin' on? Found the children yet, have you?'

Jimmy subjected him to a thoughtful look. 'Do you see any children?'

The prisoner peered over his shoulder and shook his head.

'Well then,' said the thief. 'Let's assume the obvious, shall we?'

Stump reached down to pick some grime from his toenails.

'Pity about Mick,' he said, after a while. 'I really liked him.'

'Why? What happened?'

'Well, I thought if Mick crawled through that little gap beside the slab he could probably get us some help.'

'And?'

'The slab couldn't have been properly shut. It rolled over a bit more.'

'That's terrible!' said Jimmy, shaking his head. 'Poor Mick.'

'I know,' Stump agreed. 'You thought he was small before, you should see him now.'

Jimmy suddenly put a finger to his lips.

'Did you hear that?' he said. 'Sounds like . . . I don't know, like *something*.'

Stump paused for a second, head on one side, then shrugged.

'Nah,' he said. 'It's this place, ain't it? Gets to you after a while.'

'I'm sure I heard something.'

'Could be goblins. You get a lot of goblins in places like this.'

Jimmy nodded. He wondered briefly about the rat purge in Dullitch. Perhaps the foreigner didn't drown them after all, he thought. Maybe he brought them here.

'Alloalloallo,' said Stump, who was prodding the floor with his foot. 'What's all this then?'

Jimmy looked over his shoulder.

'Have you found something?'

'Yeah, a thingy on the floor. Feels like a pedal or somethin'.' He smiled. 'Reckon I should push it?'

'Don't you?'

'I'm not too lucky with these things. Last time I pushed a pedal in the dark, I spent six months in a scorpion pit.'

'How did you get out of that one?' Jimmy asked.

'Leather soles.'

'Wow.'

'Damn right.' He checked the pedal again. 'So, do you reckon I should step on it or not?'

Jimmy looked both ways and shrugged.

'Might as well,' he said.

'What're you doing?' said Tambor.

'Well, the giant didn't take my axe away, did he?'

'Or my sword.'

'Why was that, d'you think?'

Tambor remained silent.

'Humiliation point, isn't it? He's showin' us we can't take him out even when we're armed.'

Tambor nodded.

'I see, so you're . . .'

'I'm just making the best of a bad situation.'

Gordo was scraping away at the wall with the head of his battleaxe. A few grains of dust drifted down from the brickwork.

Tambor shook his head.

'You'll never get out of a cell like that,' he said. 'People escaping from prisons by scraping away a bit at a time, it's all just stories. It doesn't actually work. Besides, how do you know this is his cave? He could've taken us to some sort of giant fortress. You could just be scraping your way into the next cell.'

Gordo stopped scraping, turned and gave the sorcerer a wry smile.

'Can you feel it?' he said.

'Feel what?'

'There's a draught coming from this wall. There's

probably a long abandoned passageway behind it.'

'Or a lot of people blowing,' said Tambor, who knew the way gods worked.

'*Grphnu*,' said Groan. He forced himself up on to his elbows. 'Where am I?'

'In the infamous cell of a thousand secreted exits,' said the sorcerer sarcastically.

'What hit me?'

'Same thing that hit me,' said Gordo.

'Here,' said the barbarian, struggling to his feet and marching over to Gordo. 'Don't bovva wiv that.'

There was a low rumble and a section of tunnel slid away.

'Well, look at that,' said Stump, standing back.

Jimmy stepped inside. The new tunnel was considerably lighter than the one they had been travelling along. It looked as if it might actually lead somewhere.

Nineteen

Nocturnals called them the Ductors, a maze of passageways and tunnels leading down into the heart of the Twelve. They were populated by all manner of mountain dwellers, most of whom were spindly creatures with lucid eyes, low on compassion but big on jewellery. It was rumoured that the mythical Greko incident took place here. (The Greko was a precious necklace owned by the gnome Johan Eegin. As the story goes, he lost the Greko to a cunning dwarf named Tablo, who outwitted him during a game of I-spy. It wasn't much of a contest, being set in the Ductors, and Tablo only managed to sneak a victory when the word 'tunnel' came up twice.)

Somewhere in the despondent darkness, a wall heaved. Behind the wall, various nocturnals scurried away.

A second concrete belch rocked the tunnel, larger this time, more weight behind it.

Then the wall crashed down.

' 'S dark,' said Groan, widening the gap in the cell by booting out a few rogue bricks around the edge. 'You got any torch spells, sorcerer?'

Tambor nodded and tried to think of the one that was hovering on the edge of his memory. It was a good torch spell, and, best of all, it didn't require fire pellets. What it *did* require was a torch, but he'd snatched one of those from the cell and had it stashed inside his robe. Still, he supposed, there was no point in bringing it out if he couldn't light it.

'The place where I bought this battleaxe from,' said Gordo. 'Bloke who sold it me reckoned it could glow in the dark.'

One after another, they stepped into the passageway. Groan blocked the opening so that they could test out Gordo's suspicion.

It was pitch dark in the tunnel.

Nothing happened.

At length, Tambor turned to the dwarf.

'Was there a low counter in the shop?' he said.

Gordo shrugged.

'Why?'

'I'm just wondering how that shopkeeper managed to see you coming.'

Groan was first to laugh at the joke, which had a lot to do with the fact that there were three of them and both of the others were involved in the telling.

'P'raps if we follow this tunnel it might lead somewhere,' he said.

'You reckon?' said Gordo, praying for strength.

They walked along in single file, Gordo leading and Groan bringing up the rear. Tambor stumbled back and forth between them.

Suddenly, a torch struck up in the darkness, bathing the tunnel in a warm glow.

Groan and Gordo started.

'Where did you get that?' said the dwarf.

Tambor's grin was so wide that it looked as if his face had split.

'In the prison,' he said. 'I just wanted to get it alight before I gave it to you.' He passed the torch to Groan and the party continued forward.

'So the old magic's coming back to your fingertips, is it?' said Gordo.

'Hah! I'm as surprised as you are. Isn't it fantastic? Memory's a wonderful thing, you know. The Naked Flame was one of the three spells I learned in my first week at the Elistalis in Dullitch. They've all but demolished the old academy now, you know.'

Gordo nodded; he'd recalled the building on his first

visit to the city. It had been a sight to behold, with its gleaming silver walls and the giant metal rings which spun endlessly on the roof.

'Shame about that, it was very, er, dominating.'

'What were the uvver two spells?' asked Groan, who was forever destined to remain half a conversation behind.

'Well,' Tambor began, biting his bottom lip. 'There was the Tower of Screaming Doom but, of course, you've seen that.' He ignored Gordo's sniggering. 'And then there was Mortis Portalitas.'

'What's that?'

'The Door of Death. That is, the opening of a dimensional portal between this realm and limbo.'

'You were taught that on your first day?'

'No, I said I learned it on my first day. In actual fact, I read it on the wall in the boys' latrine.'

'Stone me. Don't be in too much of a hurry to remember that one, will you?'

'Hah! Chance'd be a fine thing. I've practised, of course, but I've never had the nerve to actually finish the summoning.'

A little way down the tunnel Tambor noticed a small square of indentations on what he took to be the east wall. He squinted at it. The patch consisted mostly of rough lines pulled together to make a language that didn't quite sit right, no matter how you read it. It seemed as if whoever had made the markings hadn't

known how to spell the longer words properly and, instead of checking things through, had just taken his chances.

'What is it?' said Gordo. He'd walked another twenty-odd yards down the tunnel and was pretty annoyed that no one had bothered to call him back. Groan said nothing.

'It's some sort of writing. Hold on, I'm trying to translate. I think it's religious.'

They waited while Tambor felt along the scratches with his index finger.

'Mmm,' he said, after a time. 'It says that in the beginning there was a stick.'

'What kind of stick?' said Gordo. 'Did it have things coming out of it?'

'Just says a stick.'

'Was it one o' them wiv two ends?' said Groan, deep in thought.

'I don't know, it doesn't seem that important. Either that or there was a loss of concentration, because it then starts going on about a garden.' He leaned closer.

'And the gods said eat of any tree in the garden but be very careful that it is from the garden and not from anywhere else because' – he paused to catch his breath – 'just outside the garden lives a serpent who makes his own fruit with instruments we didn't give him.'

'Are you sure this is authentic?' said Gordo, frowning.

Tambor shrugged.

'How does it finish, then?' said Groan, who was getting restless.

'Er, let me see . . . oh, here, there's a prediction about the end of the world.'

Groan spat on the floor.

'Bet magic causes it,' he said.

'Don't be stupid,' Tambor snapped. 'Magic is perfectly safe in the right hands.' He went on to read about three sorcerers who wrote a magic book for children which led to the collapse of what, on Illmoor, passed for civilized society.

'It reckons a barbarian invasion will thrust the world back into the dark age,' he said.

'I thought we were in that already,' said Gordo, thoughtfully.

'It's all rubbish anyway, apart from the last bit.'

'Why, what does that say?'

Tambor squinted. 'Well, apparently, we're inside the Twelve, and it's a warning. It advises us not to venture any further unless we want to end up lost for the rest of eternity in a terrible, labyrinthine maze.'

'Hah! Load o' junk. C'mon, move,' said Groan.

They continued along the tunnel, which sloped down for a few yards and then veered sharply to the right.

'Here,' said the dwarf, suddenly stopping. Tambor practically tumbled over him.

'What is it?' said Groan.

Gordo knelt down and rubbed his hand over iron.

He checked and double-checked, then reached a conclusion.

'It's a grate,' he said. 'In the floor.'

'Can you lift it?' Tambor enquired, hopefully.

'Think so. Only one way to find out, eh?'

There followed a moment of frantic fumbling and a few mild curses when a finger got trapped. Then a scratching ensued, turned into a shaking and ended in a mad hammering. Tambor felt a chill sneak inside his robe. It started to give his legs a hard time. He felt ancient goose bumps begin to resurface.

'Hang on a minute,' said Gordo, finally. He was still down on his knees, but had apparently stopped trying to force the grate. 'It's massive.' He peered back along the tunnel. 'Groan, I reckon even you're standing on it.'

The barbarian tried to look under him and, failing to see anything, stamped his foot. There was an expansive creak.

'NOOOOO!!!!' screamed Tambor, but it was too late.

The grate fell away and the trio plummeted through the floor. Groan snatched at a broken rung but he couldn't hold on to it. The torch he'd been clutching teetered on the edge of the grate, flickered and went out.

'I've seen these before,' said Stump, looking down at a floor covered with mosaic tiles. The room seemed completely out of character against the background of the dungeon passageway. Jimmy had never seen so many bright colours, and it was extraordinarily well-lit with wall-braziers. He wondered if the gods employed a caretaker; there were certainly some very big footprints nearer the wall.

'So what's it all about?' he asked.

Stump crouched down.

'Well,' he said. 'You got to step on the right ones. If you don't you gets an arrow fly at you from them holes in the wall, there. See?'

Jimmy saw the circles and nodded. They were tiny. He shuddered; arrows that small could probably shoot right through you and you wouldn't feel it until all your bits ran out of juice.

Stump was preparing to demonstrate. He reached out and brushed a finger along the surface of the first tile. Nothing happened. He went through the same procedure with the tile next to it, and got a similar response.

'Oh well,' he said, after carrying out a spot check on a further seven surfaces. 'Maybe they're all spent or something.'

Jimmy smiled as the prisoner got up, walked into the centre of the room and collapsed with an arrow in his leg. Three more shot from the holes over his head. Stump was writhing on the mosaic tiles.

'Hold on!' Jimmy called. 'I'm coming over.'

He dropped on to his stomach and began to pull

himself towards the injured prisoner. Arrow-traps exploded above him but he reached his companion with little difficulty.

'I'm gonna pass out,' said Stump, eyes fluttering.

'Don't be ridiculous. Actually, you're very lucky; it didn't bite that far into your flesh.'

'Oh great! Thank the lords for small mercies. If I wasn't *aaahhhh—*'

Jimmy tossed the dart aside, tore off a scrap of his jerkin and dabbed away the blood on Stump's leg. Then he smiled.

'There you go.'

'I'm gonna pass out.'

'But it only bled a gnat's wing!' shouted the thief. 'You lost about a thimbleful.'

'It don't matter,' said Stump, shaking his head. 'I can't afford to lose any. Look at the size of me.'

Jimmy shook his head in amazement and crawled to the edge of the mosaic floor, dragging the prisoner after him.

'Where are we, then?' said Groan, rolling over on to his back and staring at the ceiling.

Gordo coughed.

'Hell?' he said.

'I can't see a thing,' said Tambor, nodding. 'I'm going to crawl over this way a bit. Tell me if I bump into you.'

'You'll know if you bump into Groan,' said the dwarf.

'Of course, sorry. It's the dungeon, it warps your m*iiiiiiii*—!'

There was silence.

'Tambor?' said Gordo, listening intently.

Nothing.

'Groan?'

'Yeah?'

'What happened to Tambor?'

'Dunno. I don't fink he's 'ere any more.'

The dwarf crawled around in the dark. He sounded like a pig sniffing out truffles.

'Hold on a minute,' he said finally. 'There's some sort of ahhhhhh—!'

Groan got to his feet in the darkness.

'What's this, hide 'n' seek?' he said.

He padded around the room, his back against the wall. When he'd circled it entirely, he stepped in a little and tried again. His foot caught the edge of something smooth and sloping. He dropped down on to one knee and felt it with his hands. It was a chute of some kind.

'Oi,' he shouted down it. 'You all right down there?'

There was no reply.

'All right,' he boomed. 'I'm comin' down.'

Jimmy grabbed hold of Stump's arm and pulled him back. They were about fifty yards beyond the arrow-trap room.

'Now don't tell me you can't hear *that*,' he said.

Stump put his head on one side.

'Yeah, I can.'

'What do you think it is?'

'Could be up on the mountain or somethin'.'

'No. It's closer than that. Listen properly.'

'P'raps there's a tunnel above us.'

'Could be,' said Jimmy. 'That's definitely voices, though. Don't you think?'

'Sounds like shoutin' to me, people shoutin' somethin'—'

'Listen,' Jimmy interrupted. 'It's getting nearer.'

'Hey,' said Stump, pointing towards the roof of the tunnel. 'There's a huge great hole in the ceiling.'

Jimmy looked up.

His granddad fell on him. For a second they both just lay there, frozen with shock. Then a dwarf cannoned through the same hole and landed on top of them.

Stump whistled between his teeth and shook his head.

'Blimey,' he said. 'I'm glad I weren't standin' there.'

Then Groan arrived.

Twenty

It was early morning in Dullitch and there was already a fair turnout for the big speech. Many of the citizens felt aggrieved at the prospect of having to endure life without their children. A few of them had come to give thanks.

The weather was surprisingly enthusiastic, smothering the landscape with warm sunlight, while at the same time cooling it with gentle breezes. It was looking to become one of those days, old-fashioned days, where people whistled on their way home from work and birds twittered merrily from the rooftops. At around noon picnics began to dot the lower reaches of Skulkis, transforming the tor into a patchwork of

white and green; a chessboard with brightly-coloured pawns.

In the palace, Quaris Sands was writing a speech. He was aided in the task by Duke Modeset and the troglodyte, Burnie (the only other member of the council who'd agreed to come along). Luckily, the conference room was at the top of the tallest tower and the abusive screams of the crowd were barely audible.

'There you are, milord,' said the acting chairman. He applied the final full stop and passed the speech across to Modeset, who read a few lines in each paragraph before crossing them through and scribbling over the top of them.

'Um, which bits are you changing, milord?' said Quaris, trying to ignore the glob of green slime which had just landed on the back of his hand. He threw a stern look in Burnie's direction.

'Any bits with us mentioned negatively,' Modeset replied, indicating half the page. 'I'm not sure that a fair proportion of the blame cannot be assigned to our friend Quarrell,' he said with a smile. 'He has the look of a culprit. Any chance of re-wording the speech so that most of the responsibility lies with him?'

Three floors below the conference room, Pegrand Marshall was attempting to get a Squommet out of its basket. He sat down, cross-legged, before the little creature, whistled between his teeth and waved a biscuit hopefully.

'Fizz! C'mon, Fizz, out you come.'

The shape remained dormant.

Squommets were a peculiar breed of one-winged dragon-beaver. They were incredibly furry with large teeth that extended from the base of their mouths in a sharp curve over their top lip. Fizz had been Pegrand's pet for two days and was, he had to admit, a poor example of the species. He'd bought it from a well-renowned sanctuary in Plum Hill. They had assured him of its good line, which just goes to show that excessive mating can force the hereditary gene out of any recognizable species. He'd even been shown a portrait of Fizz's parents, taken outside a hostelry near the almshouses. He looked down into the basket. Perhaps he's adopted, he thought.

Fizz stretched out a claw, tentatively at first. Then he hopped out of the basket and nuzzled across the floor. Pegrand reached down, scooped him up in his arms and went back to the basket. As usual, Fizz's paper needed changing. He lowered himself on to his haunches and picked up the dirty sheet. He was about to throw it away when he noticed there was some scribbled-out writing on it which he could just about make out. It was a letter:

Maricus Dark, Assassin
House of the Rooftop Runners
6 Palace Street
Dullitch

Dearest friend,
I wonder if you could be so kind as to help me at this
time. How long have we been friends? I wish for you
to arrange a sma—

The rest of it was either crossed through or illegible. He
held it up to the light, but still couldn't make out the
signature. Then he toyed with it pensively, running over
a number of possibilities in his head. One kept recurring.
He tossed Fizz unmercifully back into the basket, pocketed
the paper and bolted off towards the kitchens.

From his vantage point atop Karuim's Church of Holy
Origins, the assassin Mifkindle Green loaded his
patented silver crossbow, leaned over the shoulders of
two fortunately positioned gargoyles, and peered along
the shaft at his target. There was a procession going on.
This was nothing unusual; there was always a procession
going on in Dullitch. A big speech was about to be
made. An explanation to be given.

The gathering below had attracted a large percentage
of the city, which was no surprise. Among the throngs
of noblemen, merchants and market traders, Mifkindle

had already spotted Lord Bancroft, Baron Richford and Lady Terps of Pullville. He wasn't interested in any of these, however. His particular target was Duke Modeset, a man who seemed to be single-handedly responsible for the current collapse of society. He checked to ensure that the bolt was loaded before peering across at the opposite roof, to ensure that his position was being monitored by a Runners representative. The monitor waved back at him.

'Think carefully,' Pegrand urged the maid.

She'd been steadily shaking her head for the best part of ten minutes.

'I know I went up to the dining room and out to the stables,' she said, nervously. 'And then I went into town and came back and then I laid some new paper for your baby Squommet but – oh yes – I went up to see Chancellor Quarrell. He had some rubbish, I think. He's pretty scared, you know. I mean, what with the – where are you going?'

'Assassination attempt, milord!'

Modeset turned just in time to avoid Pegrand running into him.

'I beg your pardon?' he said, quickly side-stepping the manservant.

'Assassination attempt. I believe I have been fortunate enough to happen upon a copy of a letter sent to Maricus

Dark, of the Rooftop Runners Assassin network. I believe they intend to pop you off during your speech, milord.'

'I see,' said Modeset. 'Lucky for me. Any suggestions for a counter-attack?'

'Don't know, milord.'

Burnie sniffed, which didn't seem to clear anything.

'Do the people know where you'll be coming out?' he said.

Modeset nodded.

'Everyone's been told where to stand,' said Pegrand.

'Right,' said the troglodyte, cracking a knuckle somewhere in its foot. 'Then I suggest you're announced.'

'Sorry?' said Modeset, leaning towards him.

'I suggest you are announced to the crowd.'

'Who by?'

'I've got a suggestion, milord,' said Pegrand.

Fire first and ask questions later. The assassin had to admit it was a pretty lame phrase, taken at face value; but it was the only phrase by which assassins lived. Ask questions in this business and you ended up getting your answers through a medium. He peered along the crossbar and took aim.

'I assure you I—'

'Just get out there.'

'But I—'

'NOW!'

A lone figure stepped out on to the central balcony of Dullitch Palace. The crowd jeered in unison and began to pelt rotten fruit and fresh vegetables. Unfortunately none of them found their target. But an arrow did.

The crowd lapsed into silence. A woman screamed. Quarrell stared down at the ocean of faces and then up at his executioner, clutching at the arrow in his chest. Then he stumbled forward, tumbled over the balcony, and fell into the crowd.

The assassin's face became a mask of fascinated horror and he flashed a quick glance across the rooftops at his colleague, whose instinctive reaction had been to dash off towards the stairwell. He froze with fear. No assassin in his right mind would ever kill Chancellor Quarrell; the man was rumoured to be a high-ranking Yowler and the repercussions would be enormous! Even in the best-case scenario, he'd be facing instant dismissal.

The assassin shook his head, looked down and saw the guards. They were pouring into both the temple entrance and the entrance to the town hall across the street. He swept up his crossbow and ran.

Twenty-One

'Citizens of Dullitch,' exclaimed Duke Modeset, emerging out on to the balcony to address a stunned crowd. Pegrand was holding a shield over his head. 'I, your current duke, and the honorary members of your city council, have come up with a solution to the peril that darkens our day. We have dispatched a hunting party to find your stolen children and bring this terrible fiend to justice. I'd just like to point out that Mr Quarrell, your honourable ex-chancellor, has been entirely ineffectual throughout these distressing times, a fact of which our city's *magnificent* assassins were evidently aware.'

He looked down and smiled at the citizens of Dullitch. They were disposing of the late chancellor by passing his body over their heads. Modeset noticed that a funeral cart had pulled up at the back of the crowd. Was it his imagination, he wondered, or did they arrive before the chancellor landed? (In fact, they did. One dark night many weeks before, a trio of thieves working with a powerful necromancer infiltrated the realm of the dead, where they smashed a windowpane in the Reaper's study and stole a brief glimpse of the Grand Order. Returning to Dullitch, they then sold what they later referred to in court as 'winning tickets' to a few selected funeral establishments.

'Oi, mister!'

The cry rang out like the call of a highly strung bird. Duke Modeset peered down as the crowd parted for a small boy with a smudge of brown hair. Supported on a wooden crutch, he had one leg and that distinctive look mastered by the downtrodden.

'Yes, young man?'

'I reckon it was you what was responsible for the rat-catcher. I 'eard you didn't pay 'im nuffin' for drownin' all o' them rats.'

'I see. And you are?'

'Tom Piddleton! I'm the orphan what escaped the evil clutches of the music man!'

'Yes, that's right: so I heard. Very convenient, wasn't it?'

The crowd, which had been about to erupt, went suddenly silent.

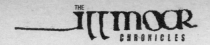

'Do what, mister?'

'I said it was very convenient – you getting away so easily.'

'Eh? I couldn't keep up. That music man, he waved his arms an' made all the other kids float on air. I was too far back, I don't think he even saw me.'

'Oh, is that right? Of course he didn't *see* you. After all, I'm certain he wouldn't have spared you your freedom out of pity. Not after leading all of our children to their certain dea . . . detainment. Isn't it more likely that he *did* see you lagging behind and decided to allow you to stagger home just so you could inform the populace of his powers and, in doing so, incite a riot. Isn't this the case? ISN'T IT SO?'

The crowd looked unsure, but they were wavering.

'I put it to you,' Modeset continued, his glare intensifying with the pitch of his voice, 'that you are nothing more than a consort of "the music man", a *hireling* returned to the city to cause civic unrest. Well, it won't work, you hear me? The good folk of Dullitch can see through such scams! I will let them judge you! Hahahahahahahah!'

Modeset flung his arms, dark-lord like, into the air and watched with unconcealed glee as the naïve majority of the crowd closed in on little Tommy Piddleton.

Behind the palace balcony, Burnie and Quaris Sands shared a worried frown.

*

After the crowd had dispersed (or, rather, after they had gathered into small groups to discuss various strikes and protests), Modeset and Pegrand returned to the conference room.

'Good showing out there, milord,' said Quaris Sands encouragingly, shaking out his robe and taking a seat at the table.

'Meanwhile,' said Burnie, 'what are we going to do about the very real possibility that we've seen the last of both the mercenaries and the thief? I mean, people are bound to be up in arms before long.'

'I have thought of a solution,' said Modeset, sternly.

'Yes, milord?'

'I suggest a concentrated digression is in order,' he said, turning to the others. 'We need to take people's mind off the crisis in hand, buy ourselves some time as it were. Therefore, I propose that we hold a fair in the palace grounds.'

'A fair, milord?'

'Yes! You know: singing, dancing, folk-music, games, etcetera. Quaris, I want you and Burnie to go to the alchemists and tell them we need to prepare a heavy-duty fireworks display. Pegrand, I want you to assemble the finest team of Morris Dancers in the city. Once we've done that, maybe—'

The troglodyte tentatively raised a claw.

'Well?'

'Er, sorry to interrupt, milord, but I'm thinking that

the alchemists might expect some sort of payment and what with the coffers empty and everything . . .'

Modeset shrugged.

'Simple. Tell them we're hunting for new barracks for the city militia and their academy looks the right size. I feel certain they'll run over each other to help. Now, get to it!'

As the group scurried from the conference room, Modeset turned and crossed over to the window, scanning the closest rooftops for assassins. Evidently, the Yowlers were becoming as restless as the general populace. It wouldn't be long before they tried again. The clock was ticking.

Twenty-Two

'Who's this I'm on?' said Groan, lifting his lower regions to enable the prisoner a gasp of air.

'That's Stump,' said Jimmy, nervously. Gordo helped Tambor to his feet and patted some dust from the sorcerer's shoulders.

Jimmy rubbed his shoulder.

'Stump, this is my granddad,' he said. 'And these are, er, his friends.'

'He ain't no friend o' mine,' said Groan, scowling.

'I'm Gordo, this is Groan,' said the dwarf, leaning against the tunnel wall.

'Never mind the introductions,' snapped Tambor. 'What the devil are you doing here, lad?'

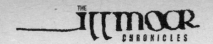

'Er, looking for you,' Jimmy lied. 'And the children.'

'What children?' said Gordo.

'The children of Dullitch,' Jimmy continued, breathlessly. 'The foreigner took them when he wasn't paid for killing the rats.'

Gordo frowned.

'Took them?' he said. 'Took them where?'

'He didn't get paid?' said Groan, who had a different set of values.

'Everyone shut up!' shouted Tambor. 'Let the boy speak.'

Four pairs of eyes fixed on the thief, who suddenly became quite timid.

'Er,' he said. 'Well, when he took the children, Duke Modeset told me to come and find you and offer you a reward to get them back—'

'How much?' said Groan.

'Shhh!'

'I'm only askin'.'

'Well don't!' snapped Gordo. 'This is serious. Being conned out of a reward is one thing, but you don't involve kiddies. That's just sick and, besides, that foreigner's not right in the head. Don't you remember when we first met him in the Ferret? His eyes were like embers and he was about ready to take on the whole bar!'

'I fort he was just daft.'

Gordo shook his head. 'That's not daft, that's suicidal.

It's like he was possessed or something.' He beckoned Groan over to one side. 'We've got to help.'

'No way,' Groan said, defiantly. 'We won't get paid.'

'We might! Anyway, it's a matter of pride. The dwarf-lords'd send out an entire army if something like this happened back home. I've got no love for the duke – I think he's a twisted sod – but, well, my brother's got two little ones.'

'I'm not goin' 'til I see some money.'

Gordo's face creased into a frown.

'Fine,' he said. 'All these years we've known each other and it comes to this, does it? I'll go on by myself, then.'

Despite the dwarf's dismissal, Groan followed him back to the group.

It was at this point that Jimmy decided, rather unwisely, to come clean about the money. 'Um,' he began. 'The duke gave me a couple of hundred crowns to give you as a down-payment. The only problem is, I sort of packed them in the horse's saddlebag and it kind of, well, ran off. Your spell-book was in there too, Granddad; sorry.'

Tambor rolled his eyes and was about to make a comment, when Gordo waved him into silence.

'Hang on,' said the dwarf. 'Let's keep focused on what's important.'

'Yeah,' snapped Groan. 'Which way did the 'orse go?'

'WHAT MAKES YOU THINK THE FOREIGNER'S UP HERE?'

'Well, we told him, didn't we?'

All eyes turned on Stump, who'd been waiting for an opening. 'Mick and I, we saw him leadin' those kids down into the depths.'

'There's got to be a path from this tunnel somewhere,' said Jimmy, ignoring the fact that both Gordo and Tambor were obviously trying to look for Mick in the darkened tunnel. 'All the others are just dead-ends.'

'Yeah,' said Stump. 'Besides, you don't fit a secret wall-panel to hide nothin'.'

Gordo shivered.

'I've heard talk of this mountain,' he said. 'They reckon the Black Horde used to meet down here somewhere. In a great big cavern, they said.'

'What Black Horde?' said Groan, who wasn't great on history.

'*The* Black Horde,' said Gordo. 'You know, in the old days. Those orcs that slaughtered a boat-load of sorcerers from Aastenglia.'

'Psst,' shouted Stump, who'd ventured a little further down the tunnel. 'I think you should see this.'

The group wandered after him, complaining about the interruption, and promptly arrived at a large gate in the centre of the passage. It intersected a two-way passage, but that wasn't what the prisoner had noticed.

The dusty floor of the tunnel was covered in footprints, hundreds of footprints. There was also a tiny sandal just off to one side.

'Ha!' said Stump. 'I told you.'

Twenty-Three

The fair wasn't proving a total success. In fact, it had started badly and was getting worse by the minute. Currently, the duke was in the throne room, casting a cursory glance over the next phase of the entertainment.

'And here they are,' said the co-ordinator, stepping aside and waving his hand indicatively. 'And I'll say this: show me a better Morris troop in all the land and you can have your money back.'

Duke Modeset cast a glance over the most pathetic assortment of miscreants he had ever set eyes on. He winced as a few of the group rushed to the aid of a member who had bent over to tie a ribbon on his leg and was having trouble standing upright again.

The duke cleared his throat.

'They're all a bit, well . . . old, aren't they?' he ventured.

The co-ordinator shrugged.

'In this case I felt only the most experienced dancers were required.'

'That one at the back with no hair, milord,' said Pegrand. 'He's on crutches, isn't he?'

'I do believe you're ri—'

'That's Mr Cribbins,' interrupted the co-ordinator, subjecting the duke's manservant to a malicious glare. 'One of the finest clappers in the district.'

Modeset gave this careful consideration.

'And he's an active member of the team, is he?'

'Oh yes, certainly, without a doubt. Unless it's Morris Dance Week, in which case he does a wonderful turn as a maypole.'

There was a moment of silence.

'I think it would be fair to suggest,' said Modeset evenly, 'that there isn't a man in this room under seventy. Am I correct?'

The co-ordinator looked around, his head bobbing and weaving to achieve an all-encompassing view.

'No, Sir,' he said eventually. 'I myself am forty-seven.'

Modeset pinched the bridge of his nose.

'Pegrand.'

'Yes, milord?'

'Hang this man from the yard-arm, will you?'

'Yes, milord. It'd be a pleasure.'

Modeset dismissed the dance troop, padded across the flagstones and collapsed into his throne. He was suffering from a terrible headache and an impending sense of doom, but at least he still had time. Oh, sure, there were rumours of heavy vandalism downtown, but that kind of thing happened all the time; nothing to worry about. The fireworks would last for another hour and after that, well, either the children would return or he'd be murdered by an army of marauding parents. In the event of the former, there was a slim chance that his life would be spared. A lengthy period of exile was likely, but nothing more. Modeset grimaced; his would certainly be a reign to remember. He gazed up at the portraits of his ancestors, and imagined that he saw a line of mocking smiles.

He was awoken from his vision by the sound of breaking glass. Pegrand came cannoning into the room and fell to his knees. His head was bleeding.

'We're under attack, milord,' he screamed. 'The palace is under attack!'

Twenty-Four

The party in the cavern were watching Groan rip out an iron gate. It didn't take long; the barbarian tossed the gate aside like a child's toy. Then he marched up to the intersection, peering cautiously in both directions.

'Anything?' Gordo enquired, battleaxe at the ready.

Groan sniffed and shook his head. 'Lot o' dust, nuffin' much else.'

Jimmy ran through the arch and knelt to study the tunnel floor.

'These footsteps came from the left, so they lead down there.'

The group turned to face the right-hand passage, which was blocked by a door of gargantuan proportions.

Exotic-looking runes were emblazoned across its surface. They shone like gold.

' 'Ere, 'old this.' Groan handed Gordo his sword, then took a run-up and charged the portal, but he couldn't budge it.

'What does the writin' say?' Stump asked, having second thoughts about his decision to stay in the mountain.

'It's the same language that was written on the wall,' Tambor told Gordo, a grimace forming. 'It says that we're nearing a place of ancient magic, a place where terrible necromancers from the first age went to die.'

'That doesn't sound good.'

'It's not. I can't imagine the dead rest easy in a place like this, and I have a feeling our foreigner is possessed by something raw, ancient and extremely terrible.'

'Sorcerers're all talk,' said Groan. 'How 'bout the door?'

Tambor shook his head.

'We'll never get through it.'

'We have to!' Jimmy exclaimed. 'Otherwise, the gods only know what he'll do to those children; they might be lost forever!'

'Look, I can only remember a handful of spells without a spell-book! Groan can't get the door open and, with respect, I'm damn sure Gordo can't. What else *can* we do but—'

There was a click, and the door creaked open. Stump was standing in front of it.

For a moment, the group just boggled at him. Finally, Gordo approached the scruffy prisoner.

'How did you do that?' he asked matter-of-factly.

'Er, well, I sort of turned the handle,' Stump admitted. 'You see, where I come from we put handles on the doors to stop people just walkin' in. Then, if you *turn* the handle like this' – he performed a small pantomime – 'the door opens. It's a proper miracle.'

Gordo tried to judge whether the prisoner was being sarcastic before deciding that, on the contrary, he was serious.

'There's a flight of stairs,' Tambor said, venturing a few feet into the passage beyond. 'Judging by the breeze, I'd say it probably opens into a cavern of some kind.'

Jimmy snapped his fingers.

'That's it,' he said. 'That's got to be it!'

Twenty-Five

A crowd of angry fathers stalked the streets. They'd split neatly into two groups; the vandalizers and the justice-seekers.

The vandalizers consisted of those fathers who worked in the building and manual trades. In a single afternoon, they'd managed to wreck the City Hall, the Treasury and a whole host of other important civic structures.

The justice-seekers, those fathers in the merchant trades who liked an ale or two, were gunning for blood.

At sunrise, they'd wanted to hurt the duke. So they demonstrated for a while, then most of them went for a small drink at the Ferret.

Lunchtime arrived, and they'd wanted to maim the

duke. So they demonstrated some more, then most of them went for a small drink at the Ferret.

After lunch, they would settle for nothing less than death, but by this time they'd had rather a lot to drink; most of them knew they wanted to kill somebody but they couldn't remember who it was.

Instead, they staggered through the streets in various stages of drunkenness, throwing stones at each other and screaming abuse. Eventually, they'd tagged along with their city-wrecking counterparts.

'Great gods,' said Quaris Sands, watching from one of the only palace windows to escape the stoning. 'The language! Is *scuddikuvoff* actually a word?'

Burnie shrugged, spilling something lumpy from one shoulder.

'I wouldn't argue with them,' he said, rolling a blobby yellow eyeball. 'This is getting out of hand, though. If those children aren't found soon, there'll be nothing for them to come home to!'

'Hear, hear.'

'So what are we going to do?'

'I don't know! The duke's all out of ideas and I'm damn sure I am.'

Quaris picked at his bushy eyebrow for a time, then appeared to reach a conclusion.

'I think,' he said, pausing between words for dramatic effect, 'that we should climb to the top of the highest tower in the palace and jump out of the window.'

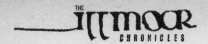

Burnie sighed.

'Very funny. We could just hide until it all blows over.'

'Hide? HIDE? We're supposed to be in charge of the city council!'

'Ha! Correction, beardy. *You* are in charge of the city council, *I* have a seat on it. Big difference. Besides, sooner or later the worst of those idiots out there are going to sober up and then they'll *really* mean business.'

'But our hands are tied! We can't do anything until we've heard from the hunting party! If there even *is* a hunting party! Oh gods! Oh despair!'

Quaris grabbed two handfuls of his own hair and dropped to his knees, emitting a low, desperate moan.

Burnie watched him with a bemused smile.

'Any chance we think about this a bit more before you book in at the clinic?'

'It's no use. We're doomed; the children are gone, the duke is going to be murdered, the city is bankrupt and we're all doomed!'

'Yes, fantastic; after you with the suicide pills. However, in the meantime, we need to keep these lunatics out of the palace, so just let me think, OK?'

'What is there to think about? We're descending into hell.'

'Yes, yes. Now, PULL YOURSELF TOGETHER!'

Quaris stopped moaning almost immediately, and struggled to his feet. After a few sniffles, he managed to regain some composure.

'Right,' Burnie continued. 'Grab some furniture and we'll try to barricade ourselves in.'

'OK, OK, but that means moving out of the shadows.'

The troglodyte twitched.

'After you.'

Twenty-Six

The party emerged out on to a rocky promontory overlooking a vast darkness. Jimmy was the first to get a clear view of his surroundings.

It wasn't a cavern, he decided, because caverns had roofs and this place just seemed to go on and on forever. He gazed around him in awe, feeling like a tiny insect staring up at the universe for the first time. Above, and to either side, there was darkness. Below, there were . . . children.

They congregated on the cavern floor. There were hundreds of them, yet they barely made a dent on the vast expanse. Jimmy suspected that you could probably enter the cavern from the other side and walk right past them without spotting them on your way out again.

Groan Teethgrit shook his head in disbelief.

'I fort I'd seen ev'ry cavern in Illmoor,' he said. 'Don't 'member this one.'

'Fair bet you've seen every tavern in Illmoor,' said Gordo, grinning.

'I don't like the look of this place,' said Jimmy. 'It's a bit . . . distorted.'

'There he is,' said Tambor, pointing across the cavern.

Diek Wustapha stood atop a large boulder amidst the juvenile sea. He was absolutely still.

'Maybe we could sneak the children out,' Jimmy ventured. 'There's enough caves down there. One of them must lead to the surface, law of averages. What d'you reckon? I could try it, quiet like. Besides, it doesn't look as if he's awake.'

'He's awake,' said Tambor, eyes narrowing. He looked down at the children who were milling around far below. They were sleepwalking, but they would only get so far before they turned back and stumbled in the opposite direction, as if repelled by some invisible wall of force.

'Oi!' said Groan, suddenly. 'Look at 'im!'

A circle of light had formed in the air above Diek Wustapha. It descended on him, swirling around his torso and extending outwards, sweating a dark yellow light. Gordo hefted his battleaxe and took aim, but Tambor pulled him back.

'That's dark magic,' he said sternly. 'You've got no hope, trust me.'

'What can we do, then?' said Groan, who didn't like the look of it either.

Jimmy peered over the lip of the protruding rock. It was a fair way down, he had to admit. The City Hall precipice all over again. He weighed up his chances of landing safely, then realized it probably didn't matter how he landed. If the ground didn't kill him, the foreigner would.

'I reckon I could get the children out now,' he lied, looking at his granddad evenly.

'I can probably help, there,' said Stump, with a lopsided grin. 'I'm good with kids. I've got twenty-six from my first marriage.'

'Damn,' said Groan and Gordo in unison, looking at the prisoner with a sudden respect.

'That leaves *us* with the foreigner,' Tambor said to them, rolling up his sleeves. 'Right.'

Gordo noticed the old man's expression and closed a podgy hand over his wrist.

'Hold on, Tambor. What're you doing?'

'A spell.'

'Not the Tower of Screaming Doom, surely?' Gordo's eyes rolled back in his head. 'What good's that going to do here?'

Groan sniffed. 'He might die laughin'.'

The dwarf made to chuckle, but Tambor's expression stopped him dead.

'I'm going to try the Doorway of Death.'

'But, but . . . but you don't have your spell-book!' shouted Jimmy, wide-eyed.

'I don't need it, I think I can remember.'

'But you can't fight him with magic, Granddad. Not *him*. He's in league with something awful.'

'I don't plan to *fight* him,' said Tambor. 'I'm going to try to open the portal behind him. I think it's just like a fissure in time. Somebody else will have to push him inside.'

'Leave that to us,' Gordo said. He turned to Jimmy and Stump. 'You get those kiddies out.'

Jimmy nodded and peered over the edge of the promontory. Then he seemed to reach a decision. He took a few steps back, closed his eyes and jumped. He would have landed perfectly had he remembered to open them again.

'Agggghhh.'

Tambor rushed to the edge.

'You all right?' he shouted down.

'Fine,' came the reply. 'Just got a bit of a pain in the ar*hhhh*.'

'What?'

'It's all right. I hit my head getting up.'

'Great,' Gordo whispered to Groan. 'If he didn't know we were here before, he knows now.'

'I heard that,' said Tambor, scowling at the mercenaries. 'Jimmy's a brave lad.'

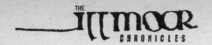

'Oh, he is,' said Gordo, reassuringly.

It was Groan's turn to go over the edge. He unhooked a leather knapsack, which nobody had noticed before, and pulled a length of rope from inside.

'Where the hell did you get that from?' shouted Tambor.

Groan shrugged.

'Always carry rope,' he said. 'Never know when it'll come in 'andy.'

'Why didn't you say you had that before Jimmy jumped?'

'You didn' ask. 'Ere, Gordo, you comin'?'

He fastened the rope around a tiny ledge above the mouth of the cave and began to abseil over the lip of the rock. The dwarf waited a while, then followed him. Stump waited in the shadows, wondering which course of action would turn out to be the best bet.

Tambor shook his head clear of thoughts, straightened up and returned his attention to the foreigner. Then he mumbled a few syllables and breathed a smoke ring through his nose. It floated in the air above him for a time, then became a thin wisp of green. Finally, it descended. As it curled around the foreigner, a strange light filled his eyes.

On the ground, Gordo, Groan and Jimmy Quickstint had stumbled upon a problem.

'It's an invisible wall,' said Gordo. He took a step

back and swung his battleaxe at it. There was a glancing 'crack', but nothing happened.

'Great,' said Jimmy, rolling his eyes.

'Le' me 'ave a go,' said Groan, putting his weight against the barrier.

'Paid good money for this axe,' Gordo muttered to himself. 'The bloke told me it'd go through magic barriers like a knife through butter – no problem, he said.'

Groan had failed to shift the unseen boundary. Instead, he was taking out his frustration on a nearby rock.

'Maybe there's some way over it,' Jimmy hazarded.

'He said to me, Gordo, why would I sell you rubbish when you're practically family and I said—'

'Stan' back,' said Groan. He picked up the rock he'd been jumping up and down on, reeled back and hurled it at the wall. It smashed into pieces.

'He's got those kids mesmerized,' said Jimmy, staring into the circle. 'Look at 'em. We've got to do something quick.'

'What about a dagger, they said. Dwarves *should* have a dagger, but I said—'

'Will you shut up about that stupid axe!' Jimmy screamed.

Then a bolt of energy pierced the circle.

Jimmy looked up.

'It's Tambor,' said Gordo, following the beam to the

sorcerer's fingertips. 'It must be part of the doorway spell. Why couldn't he have remembered that one in the wood?'

Groan had chosen to take a running leap at the invisible barricade. This time (to his considerable surprise) he crashed right through it, bowling over a few of the children.

Diek Wustapha's eyes flicked open.

'He's awake!' screamed Jimmy.

The dwarf looked up.

'Quick!' he shouted. 'Find another exit.'

All across the floor, eyes blinked and heads shook. The children were waking up. There was sobbing, crying, foul exclamations and an awful lot of bewilderment. One or two of the more astute kids were already picking up stones as if, in true Dullitch spirit, they could smell a kick-off brewing.

Stump was feeling his way along the east wall of the cavern, hunting for a different set of steps. The foreigner *had* to have walked them down somehow.

'Over there,' came a shout from Jimmy. He was pointing at an arch further along the same wall section, a toddler clutched in his other arm. 'We'll take them that way. It must join the tunnel where they came in.'

'You go on,' Stump shouted. 'I'm gonna see if I can find a back-up route in case that one turns out to be a dead-end. Be careful, though, this place is riddled with hooooooooooollllleeeeeeesss—'

Jimmy gasped; the prisoner had disappeared right in front of him. There was a muffled cry, becoming more distant as it progressed and, finally, it stopped. Jimmy didn't reckon he'd see the prisoner again.

Diek Wustapha looked down at the children.

Don't let them leave, boy. Focus your mind, control them.

He closed his eyes and turned his palms outward. A few rogue vapours swam away on the wind, but then there was nothing. The children were no longer responding to his thoughts. He reached for the flute.

Forget that foolish toy, Diek. It's nothing; you don't need it. Watch now, see what you can do on your own . . .

Diek gasped; a blue mist had emanated from his fingertips. It rose, hung on the air and then plunged into the cavern floor.

For a moment, nothing happened.

Then the ground started to shake.

Well done, Diek. Well done. For now, we have our own friends to help us . . .

Twenty-Seven

Duke Modeset stood atop the tallest tower of his palace, surveying the rebellion below through an elegant telescopic device he'd found in the war room.

His manservant stood a little way behind him, looking uncomfortable.

'Sorry to keep on, milord, but why am I standing on this trapdoor, again?'

The duke sighed.

'I've told you, Pegrand, in order to keep our most energetic citizen from running me through with a blade.'

'But I've locked it, milord, and I've jammed a crowbar through the handle.'

'Yes, well, I'm not taking any chances. Now, just stand still, will you?'

'Er . . . right, milord. Whatever you say.'

Modeset returned his attention to the telescope, then folded it away.

'We're in big trouble this time, old friend. You do realize that, even if the children miraculously come hurtling through the gates in the next five minutes, my days in this city are numbered?'

'Oh, no, milord. Surely if—'

Modeset waved his manservant's protestations away.

'We have to face facts, Pegrand. Even if the parents forgive me, the Yowlers won't give up an opportunity to step in. They've wanted my blasted cousin for the throne ever since he was born. If I don't get murdered, at the very least I'll be put into exile. Perhaps it might be best for all concerned if I just jump.'

Modeset climbed up on to the nearest buttress and stretched out his arms like a man imitating a bird.

'B-b-but you can't—'

A sword blade suddenly shot up through the trapdoor, narrowly missing the manservant's privates.

'Um, right you are, milord,' he gasped. 'Don't hang about, now.'

Twenty-Eight

The cavern was a hive of frantic activity. Children scrambled left and right, dodging and swerving to avoid the walking cadavers Diek had enticed from the cracked earth in an attempt to stop them leaving.

'Down! Down! Dooowwwwnnnn!'

Gordo flew over the heads of the nearest children as if he'd been fired from a cannon, barrelling into the undead mass with his battleaxe a blur. Skulls shattered and half-rotted limbs flew left and right, but the dwarf wasn't having things all his own way. An evil-looking gash had been opened on his forehead and several of the staggering grave-walkers were clawing mindlessly at his back. With every triumphant blow, he darted frantic glances left and right, but Groan was nowhere to be seen.

Kill the sorcerer, boy. Destroy him.

Diek tried to focus his gaze on Tambor. This time, a plume of yellow fire flew from his hands and surged towards the sorcerer. It hit the rocky ledge beneath him which in turn came away from the wall and crashed to the ground.

Diek smiled with satisfaction, and tried again. A furious bolt of energy flew across the cavern, encased the old man and spun him around in mid-air, increasing in velocity until Tambor was nothing more than a blur. The spell intensified and the air began to hum. One more effort and ... he toppled backwards.

The boulder had moved. Diek peered over his shoulder, and saw the barbarian grinning up at him.

Groan was underneath the boy's temporary stage, employing his considerable strength to tip it up. He gave one final grunt of effort, and Diek fell. The spell was broken.

Tambor plummeted. He still had the awareness to roll as he hit the ground, but his own momentum took him over the edge of the promontory. His legs scrabbled for purchase on the rock face and he hung there, dangling precariously in mid-air.

*

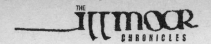

Thanks to some lucky hacks and a small group of enthusiastic, rock-pelting teenagers, Gordo was winning his battle with the undead. Cutting down the last hideous corpse in his path, he paused to catch his breath before rounding up the remaining innocents. Not that there were many; the children had evidently decided pretty quickly that they didn't like the place they'd woken up in, and most of them had already begun to follow Jimmy towards the exit tunnel.

It was just as well; things were about to get a lot worse.

Tambor had managed to scrabble back on to his ledge. He got shakily to his feet and patted the dust from his robe. I'm too old for this, he thought, as he lowered himself down on to one creaky knee and began to recite his chant.

'Come on, you stragglers! Get through the tunnel!'

Gordo sighed; being three foot nothing didn't prepare you well for ordering children to follow you.

Further along, Jimmy was having his *own* trouble maintaining order. He'd realized early on that the easiest way to control the situation would be to occasionally grab one kid, issue an instruction and hope for the best. He reached out and grasped a jerkin.

'Hurry along,' he snapped. 'There's a . . . a terrible five-headed troll coming.'

He looked down. A little girl with pigtails was trembling.

*

Calm down.

Diek was trying to dislodge the voice from his skull. He clapped his hands over his ears and screamed.

CALM DOWN.

He dropped to the ground, eyes suddenly devoid of soul.

Now focus on the rock.

Groan wondered if the foreigner was lying behind the boulder, unconscious. He hoped he was. With an almighty effort, he put tremendous pressure on the rock and moved it forward a few feet. Then he let go, leaped back and grimaced. The boulder was rolling towards him again, fast. He turned and ran.

Jimmy was having a hard time. He'd finally managed to assure the little girl with pigtails that, no, there *wasn't* a terrible five-headed troll coming, but that they did still need to hurry. He'd carried her to the head of the line but had to put her down again because, surprisingly for a little thing with not an ounce of fat on her, she'd weighed a ton.

'QUIETEN DOWN!' he boomed. A few sniggers broke out about twenty heads down the line.

'Ummy says you shudden shout at children,' said the little girl.

Jimmy raised one eyebrow.

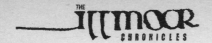

'Ummy's not trapped inside a mountain,' he said, then stopped abruptly. He'd expected a few surprises, coming out of a mountain with thousands of children. A portcullis hadn't been one of them.

It ran from wall to wall and blocked the path from floor to ceiling. He felt around for a lever but couldn't find one. He turned back to the girl.

'Does 'ummy have anything to say on the subject of subterranean portcullises?' he asked.

'Dunno,' said the girl. She sniffed. 'Don't fink she's interested in that.'

No, thought Jimmy, I bet she isn't.

'Right,' he said. 'Stand back. I'm going to lift it.'

He reached down and took hold of two squares in the iron. Then he pulled with all his might. Nothing happened. A few small boys hurried up to help, but there was just no moving the thing.

Jimmy sighed.

'OK everyone,' he started. 'We'll have to go ba—'

'We *will* not.'

Gordo appeared from behind the knees of a gangly teenager, and nudged his way up to the group at the portcullis.

'Let's move this thing, shall we?' he said.

The dwarf clasped gnarled hands around the squares on the grid, and began to haul with all his might. Again, a few eager teens lent some dubious assistance. At last, there was a slow and dreary creak. Then the portcullis began to grind upwards. A small boy near the front cheered and clapped his hands. He was soon joined by others. Gordo didn't know why but, somehow, this made him feel about three inches taller.

'There's not much space,' he breathed. 'You, the girl with the pigtails, go through and see if there's a button you can push to lock this thing.'

Despite Jimmy's protests, the little girl stepped forward. Then she hesitated.

'Ummy says—'

'I don't care. Just GET THROUGH AND DO IT.'

The girl crouched down and crawled through the gap.

A few seconds later there followed a sharp click. It echoed off through the tunnel. Gordo breathed a sigh of relief and let go. The portcullis slid down again.

The rock had caught up with Groan Teethgrit and wedged the barbarian into a corner. He heaved at it but the magical force driving it on was simply too powerful.

Tambor was halfway through his chant when he first consciously realized the power of the spell he was about to perform. This was no mere conjuration, *this was the Doorway of Death*. Once you'd cast it, there was definitely no going back. He didn't even know what was likely to happen, only that it might involve him ... paying a price. Back in his days at the Elistalis, he'd heard plenty of the older pupils talking about it, and most of the

fractured conversations he'd caught were worrying. Some said that a terrible creature arrived to claim the victim, while others warned that even the act of invoking the spell drained the life from the caster. Tambor gulped; that was a possibility he was just going to have to entertain. He began to invoke the last line of the chant.

On reflection, it hadn't been a bad old life really, full of exciting quests and astounding magical discoveries in the early days, full of . . . er . . . paperwork afterwards. He came to the end of the spell, stopped, and felt the magic surge through him.

He pointed a finger at Diek Wustapha and prayed.

It happened almost immediately.

There was a thunderclap, which resonated deep inside the base of the cavern, and a seam tore in the fabric of reality. Tambor gasped; he'd misjudged his positioning, and the portal hovered a short distance behind the foreigner, who was facing away from it, oblivious.

Maybe, thought Tambor, he'll just step back and stumble straight into it. He smiled wanly; it was wishful thinking, and he knew it.

Diek was raising the pressure on Groan, face contorted with the gut-wrenching effort required to steer the magic in his mind.

Tambor took a deep breath, steeled himself and began to climb down from his ledge to the cavern floor.

*

'What's the hold-up?' shouted Jimmy, trying to peer past Gordo into the shadows beyond the portcullis. The dwarf had managed to lift the great gate once more, but he was groaning with the effort involved.

'Pigtails reckons she can't press the button properly,' he called. 'She's not tall enough. I know the feeling.'

'I'll do it,' said Jimmy, scrambling under the spikes that stabbed from the underside of the barrier. A click echoed through the tunnel, but this time Gordo waited a few seconds. Then he released his grip on the iron and stepped away. Mercifully, the portcullis stayed where it was.

Jimmy scrambled back through the gap.

'See?' he said. 'No problem. There might be a way out, too. She can see a light.'

'Good.'

Gordo turned back towards the congregation of faces.

'Everyone follow me!' he shouted, and ducked under the portcullis.

'Right,' said Jimmy. 'I'm going back a bit to make sure we've got them all. Hopefully, we'll meet up again out in the open.'

Groan Teethgrit heaved at the boulder, but Diek's unshakable concentration was closing the gap, fast. He felt as if he was trapped in a vice powered by the gods. The harder he fought, the more the pressure built, squashing, squeezing, crushing, until . . .

... it stopped, suddenly and without any apparent victory on Groan's part. The barbarian eased himself from his crevice and lurched forward to see what had happened.

There was a fight going on.

From what little Groan could make out through the swirls of magic still crackling in the air, Tambor had barrelled into the foreigner and was currently belting seven bells out of him with a bruised (but nevertheless effective) closed fist. The boy's face was progressing through a series of strange attitudes and he looked both frightened and furious. As Groan headed towards the scuffle, Diek shot up an arm which coursed with energy and sent the old man careering back across the cavern. He gazed admiringly at his own hands and flashed the approaching barbarian an otherworldly smile.

Good, Diek. Very good. You see? These people are no match for you.

Groan drew his sword, swung it back in a wild arc and let go.

Diek caught the blade in mid-air, and tossed it aside. '*Is that the best you can do?*' he asked, his voice now edged with a disconcerting lilt.

Tambor struggled to his feet, screamed in frustration and charged.

Diek gave an evil cackle, and stepped aside, but he was a fraction too late to avoid contact completely. Tambor flew past, catching the boy a heavy blow on the side of the head before he disappeared into the dark doorway amidst a flurry of curses. There was a loud roar from beyond. The portal sizzled, as if in the process of digesting the old sorcerer. Then it began to close.

But Diek had lost his concentration. He staggered, reeling from the old man's blow, clutching his skull and moaning.

He didn't see Groan.

The barbarian bolted across the cavern, muscle-racked legs pumping with furious energy. He reached the foreigner, snatched him up by the neck and hurled him at the shrinking darkness.

Diek awoke from his reverie just in time to snake out a hand and grab the edge of the doorway, but it was too late.

The portal closed . . . and the cavern fell silent.

The last wisp of stray magic faded away. Groan stood ready to fight, one eye on the space previously occupied by Tambor's Doorway. I've gotta get myself a bigger sword, he thought.

Twenty-Nine

'Goodbye Dullitch! May all your future monarchs suffer
the same hellish, vomitous luck that I've had to endure.'

Modeset tilted forward on tiptoe, allowed himself one
final glimpse of the city and dropped . . .

. . . down . . .

. . . down . . .

. . . down . . .

At this point, somewhere past the third floor, he
landed on a flagpole which propelled him back up at an
alarming speed. He subsequently erupted through the
wooden floor of a balcony on the fourth, crashed the
wrong way through its awning, clung frantically to the
tattered remains of the same, swung into the palace like

a crazed monkey and landed face first on the floor of the throne room before Quaris Sands and Burnie.

'Nice of you to drop by, milord,' said the troglodyte, ducking a brick which had followed the duke in. 'At least you're doing your bit to keep the crowd entertained.'

There followed an inevitable outburst of derisive laughter, punctuated by some serious blasphemy from the bruised duke. This petered out when the throne-room door came crashing down, and a sea of crazed parents poured in through the gap.

Thirty

Somehow, due to a strange conjunction of circumstances, Gordo found himself playing catch-up. Since leaving the mountain, he appeared to have lost the initiative. Children milled around him, pushing and shoving (in some cases without so much as an apology). It seemed as though, via some basic instinct, they knew the way home. Perhaps, Gordo thought, you log stuff on some higher level when you're in a trance. Remarkable.

Jimmy caught up with him.

'Bit of luck, that portcullis coming up easy,' he said.

The dwarf scowled.

'It wasn't luck and it wasn't easy! It was strength, boy. Never judge a man by his size.'

'Strength? You think?'

'Yes. Do you want to make something of it?'

'No, of course not.' Jimmy held up his hands in surrender. 'I just wouldn't've thought it, that's all. You must be very, er, able.'

Gordo nodded.

'You ever hear of the time when Groan defeated the seven-headed dragon of Anzell Bay?'

'Hmm . . . I think so,' Jimmy lied.

'I ripped the claws off it when he'd finished.'

'Amazing,' the thief muttered. 'I bet that took some doing.'

'Ha! It's no fun, I can tell you, manicuring a dragon. Grime gets right under your fingernails.'

'No, I'm sure. Have you seen Stump, by any chance?'

'Your mate with all the hair? I thought he was with you.'

Jimmy shook his head. 'He fell down a chute or something.'

'Ha! Silly sod. He'll be in that mountain for weeks!'

'Oi,' shouted a voice.

Gordo and Jimmy turned to see Groan emerging from the tunnel. The barbarian looked battered, bruised and miserable. At least *he's* unaffected, thought Gordo. As the barbarian approached, Jimmy looked around him.

'Where's Granddad?' he called.

There was a dreadful, dreadful silence.

''E's gone,' Groan managed, at last. 'Sorry.'

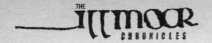

Jimmy shook his head.

'What do you mean "gone"?' he asked, fighting back the first hint of a tear. 'Where? How?'

Groan took a while to answer.

'He went fru the doorway, took the foreigner wiv him.'

'He was a brave man,' lied Gordo, patting the thief affectionately on the leg. 'Those children may very well owe their lives to him.'

'And us,' added Groan, who was prepared to go so far with a lie, but didn't want any sentimental issues interfering with his share of the reward.

A wind whistled on the mountainside.

'Looks like the children can't wait to get back,' said Jimmy, trying not to show his sorrow. He was gesturing towards a group of thirty or forty youths who had wandered off the path to start a rock-fight between the trees. 'Bless them, eh?'

'Little demons,' Gordo snapped.

'City owes us money,' said Groan, with rancour.

Jimmy smiled at the thought of Modeset parting with gold; perhaps Dullitch's purse-string vigilante wasn't going to get away without a scratch, after all.

'I wish I hadn't lost that horse,' he said.

'So do we,' Gordo muttered.

The thief shook his head. 'No, I meant for the ride home.'

'I like walkin',' said Groan. 'More chance of a fight.'

'Me too,' added Gordo. 'Nice fresh air in your lungs.' He licked his lips. 'I expect you'll be in for your granddad's fortune,' he said, grinning. 'The spell-book, that is.'

Jimmy sniffed, nodded.

'Not my thing,' he said. 'There isn't a magical bone in my body, thank the gods.'

They walked in silence for a while.

'Of course,' Jimmy added, thoughtfully. 'There *was* always his gold Vortiga bracelet. That must be worth thousands.'

There was another prolonged suppression of breath.

'You'll be after that, then?' said Gordo, slyly. 'You being a thief and all.'

Jimmy shook his head.

'Not likely.' He passed a grubby hand over his forehead. 'He never wore it, but he always had it on him somewhere. In a pocket, under his hat, in a shoe; anywhere you'd care to mention. Personally, I reckon he used to hide it inside that magic carpet of his.'

Groan looked up towards the summit of the Twelve, and wondered if it was worth going back.

Thirty-One

The parents had sticks, cudgels, knuckle-dusters and, in one extreme case, a knife. And yet they didn't move an inch towards the duke. They didn't dare.

Vicious had emerged from beneath the royal throne and proceeded, very quickly, to go off his rocker. Unbeknownst to the duke, who thought the little mutt might actually be displaying some deep sense of loyalty, he was actually protecting his bone. The hideous, half-rotted thing was hidden underneath a collapsed tapestry just behind the door, and one of the parents had taken a step in the wrong direction. It wasn't the growl that frightened them, because Vicious didn't growl. Instead, he made a noise like a yodeller gargling with acid, his eyeballs rolling right back into his head, spit flying from his maw in every direction.

Every weapon clattered to the floor.

The duke, who had finally mustered enough dignity to scramble to his feet, raised a shaking hand.

'I understand you people want some answers,' he began. 'But the fact is, I have none to give you. Myself and my officials' – he indicated Quaris and Burnie who both gave very weak waves – 'have done the best we can in the circumstances. Now, will you please go to your homes and await the return of your children. Or else, I will . . . give the command.'

Hesitation.

Doubt.

Defiance.

Then there was a series of mumbled discussions and, one by one, the parents began to shuffle from the room.

When the last of them had departed, Modeset breathed a sigh of relief and, stepping forward, carefully patted his little dog.

'Thank you for that, my friend,' he said, turning back to the others. 'You know, I think he understands—'

What happened next, happened in a blur. One moment the dog was sitting beside Modeset, wagging its tail excitedly, and the next it was hanging off his throat.

Thirty-Two

So the children of Dullitch returned, just in time for the duke – and there was much rejoicing. The streets were filled with thankful parents, happy sons and joyful daughters. Quaris Sands threaded his way through the crowds, shaking hands with some of the fathers and winking at their excitable offspring in that patronising way that only adults with no children seem to employ.

In the palace, Groan and Gordo were also getting the red carpet treatment. Strangely, they'd been prevented from entering the city through the main gate with the children. Instead, a group of guards had taken them, via a very strangled route, to the palace.

Now, they stood before the duke who, it seemed, was

wearing some sort of padded collar-support.

'The city of Dullitch is in your debt,' Modeset announced, pouring two measures from an expensive-looking bottle and passing the flagons to Pegrand to distribute. 'You shall receive a full pardon, and the freedom of Dullitch.'

'We'd bedda,' Groan muttered, snatching his drink and scowling at the duke's manservant. 'I've 'ad a gutful o' this stinkin' city. Where's our money?'

Modeset edged his way around the desk.

'What are you talking about? I gave Quickstint a thousand crowns!'

'Hah!' Gordo was first off the mark. 'We never got that – the thief lost the horse before he found us. We haven't seen a single crown of your damn money!'

Modeset gave an impassive shrug.

'I don't see how that's my problem.'

'Oh, you don't? Maybe Groan and I should show you.'

The duke began to twitch.

'Where is the horse now?' he asked.

'That's it! I've had enough.'

Gordo took one last swig from his flagon and tossed it aside.

'Come, come,' Modeset soothed. 'There's no need to get excited, little fellow. It was merely a question.'

'Yeah,' Groan boomed, 'and this is *merely* a sword, but it's *nearly* stickin' out the back of your bleedin' 'ead.'

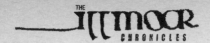

The duke flinched, but suddenly his confidence seemed to strengthen.

'Oh really?' he snapped. 'Then step up, great warrior, for it seems we have little to talk about.'

The hulking barbarian drew his blade, took a stride forward, staggered, and collapsed. The flagon clanked across the marble floor, spilling its contents.

Gordo watched his friend in amazement, but found himself too weary to help. His limbs felt like lead weights.

'Now!' Modeset cried.

Pegrand hurried over to the door, where a rope snaked through a heavy torch bracket. He yanked the knot free and a great iron cage clanked down over the two mercenaries.

Burnie the troglodyte struggled out from the tattered remains of the great palace curtains. He was holding a small glass phial.

'We can't hang around,' he said. 'The alchemists reckon these sleeping draughts never last more than a couple of hours.'

'Very good. Pegrand, Quaris and I will take the barbarian. Burnie, do you think you can manage the dwarf?'

'Just about.'

'Right, then. To the dungeons!'

Thirty-Three

Gordo Goldeaxe was drowning his sorrows with some ale he'd found in a dank corner of his cell. At least, it tasted like ale. He held the bottle up and regarded it, critically. It certainly *was* a strange colour. He had a feeling it was watered down or low on liquor content. Either way, it was totally failing to get him drunk.

A few seconds passed in silence. Outside, a half-moon glowed in the sky. Gordo put his feet up on the bench beside him. He was about to nod off when a tune rang out from the next cell.

'Is that you, Groan Teethgrit?'

'Yeah.'

'What is it?'

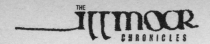
''S a flute.'

'Where did you get that?'

'Fell outta the foreigner's robe when I 'ad ' im off the rock.'

Gordo leapt off his bunk.

'Throw it away,' he shouted. 'It's probably cursed.'

'Wants to be,' said Groan, continuing to produce a strangled tune from it. 'I've a good mind to try an' get them rats back.'

'If he didn't kill them,' said Gordo, unhelpfully. 'I hate this city. It's a flaming cesspit. These cells are like sewers.'

'Fick walls, 'n'all,' said Groan. 'I spent a year tryin' to get out of 'ere once; no good, hard as iron. These dungeons run right under the road.'

Clip clop. Clip clop.

Clip clop, clip clop.

It was coming from above. Gordo looked up to the roof grate, but he couldn't see anything but moonlight and shadows.

Clip clop.

Clop.

Clop.

Gordo jumped up and down, stretched left and right, but he still couldn't make anything out. In the next cell, Groan was up and padding across the stones.

''Ere,' said the low booming voice, after a time.

Gordo sighed. 'What? What is it?'

'You 'member that 'orse the thief lost?'

'Of course! I'm hardly likely to forget it, am I?'

'It's standing in the street over my cell!'

'Don't be ridiculous.'

'Well, it *looks* like an 'eraldic horse to me. 'S got a fat saddlebag 'n'all.'

'You don't seriously think it's the same animal!'

'Dunno. I reckon it might be a homin' horse. You know what I mean, one that comes back on its own accordian.'

'Well, there's nothing we can do about it now,' said Gordo doubtfully, and settled down to sleep.

Eventually, around midnight, Groan stopped trying to coax the horse within reach and took a nap himself. He dreamed of beautiful maidens, a bath full of soya milk and a scrubbing brush. In that order.

Thirty-Four

The following morning, as Jimmy Quickstint entered the draughty chambers beneath Yowler House, several high-ranking dignitaries stared out at him from the depths of their swarthy hoods. The halls here were lined with fanciful brocades, all hand-stolen from many of the wealthiest lords in Dullitch.

In the centre of the room sat Riggor DeWatt, master of the Rooftop Runners for more than forty years. His face, like those of his colleagues, was concealed, but he wore a ring of such magnificence that his identity was obvious. It actually required two fingers to support it.

Jimmy reached the centre of the chamber, and bowed low.

'You asked to see me, sir?'

The hood looked up. Jimmy could just make out the shadowy form of a chin.

'I did,' came a booming, resonant voice. 'Jimmy Quickstint—'

'Yes, sir?'

'Quiet! Jimmy Quickstint—'

'Sir?'

'Silence! I'm trying to pronounce you. JIMMY QUICKSTINT—'

The thief tried to avert his eyes, while at the same time looking hopeful.

'Because of your bravery—'

'My bravery?'

'*Your bravery*,' echoed the congregation of cowls.

'Your honour—'

'Honour? Really?'

'*Your honour.*'

'And your loyalty to the crown.'

'*To the crown.*'

There was a pause.

'We have decided against admitting you to our organization. Sadly, we do not think that honour, bravery or loyalty in this arena are directions in which we feel bound to move. Please leave via the west door, depositing your yearbook and complimentary swag-bag in the alcove provided. If you don't have these items about your person, you are advised that you are gifted

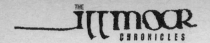

with one week of five days to return them. You also, it
seems, owe the city a thousand crowns, so we strongly
suggest you begin your search for the royal steed
immediately. Good day.'

Jimmy raised a hand to protest, but he was suddenly
snatched and frog-marched, by the elbows, out of a
nearby door. Before he could so much as kick out a leg,
he was dragged along a draughty passageway, hauled up
several flights of stairs and deposited, face first, on the
cold cobbles of Palace Street, where he lay in a crumpled
heap, too tired to move and too depressed to think.
After a couple of seconds an alley cat padded up to him
and widdled in his ear.

Epilogue

Duke Modeset stood trial for his 'incompetent handling' of the series of events which subsequently came to be known as 'The Ratastrophe Catastrophe'. He was exiled, along with his trusted manservant, Pegrand, leaving the throne to one Viscount Curfew, a rather insipid young man whom the Yowlers were rumoured to have firmly in their pocket. Under his reign, the city once again became a haven for thieves and assassins, but at least the children were safe (a silver statue of Diek Wustapha was placed in the Market Square to ensure that they always behaved themselves).

Duke Modeset's expulsion did not mark the end of his relationship with Dullitch, however, for he would

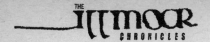

return, some seven years later, at a time when the city faced an even greater crisis . . .

About the Author

David Lee Stone was born in Margate Hospital on 25th January, 1978. He was educated badly and therefore cannot by law name any of the schools at which this occurred (though one of them actually burned down before being relocated somewhere else).

After leaving school, David worked as a customer services rep at a well-known retail outlet and helped to financially bankrupt his mother's (then successful) estate agency before searching for employment elsewhere. During this time he also began to contribute stories and/or review columns to a variety of different magazines including *Interzone*, *Xenos*, *The Edge*, Games Workshop's *Citadel Journal* and Future Publishing's *SFX* (for whom he still works). In 1997, the first 'Dullitch' short story was accepted and published in *Knights of Madness*, an anthology that appeared in hardback and paperback on both sides of the Atlantic.

These days, David can usually be found hammering away at a keyboard somewhere along the swollen lip of Kent.

The Ratastrophe Catastrophe is the first novel of the Illmoor Chronicles. The next in the series is currently underway.

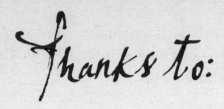

Thanks to:

My mother; apart from giving me overwhelming support and encouragement since I began writing, she has patiently read and re-read every chapter of this novel since it was started in 1996. She also found me the best agent in the business. Sophie Hicks, that very agent, for unswerving support and a faith that never faltered. My editor, Venetia Gosling, for her incredible enthusiasm for Illmoor and her exhaustive patience with its author. My family have also been terrific, in particular my inimitable grandmother, Doris Christina Ford, and John 'Mick' Ford, a giant among uncles. Last but not least, thanks to Lee Andrews, Rita and Stephen Copestake, Peter Haining, Anne McNeil, Honor Wilson-Fletcher, my late father, Henry 'Harry' Cooke and my wonderfully supportive girlfriend, Chiara Tripodi.

If you liked The Ratastrophe Catastrophe, you'll love the next instalment of the Illmoor Chronicles – The Yowler Foul-up . . .

One

. . . Somewhere in the north-eastern corner of the forest, a tiny sprite emerged from the gloomy depths of a tree hollow and listened, translucent wings fluttering in the mid-morning breeze. A boot crushed it into the wood.

The thief was out of breath. He had run the length of Grinswood in just under three hours, which was a boastful feat for a man on horseback, let alone one with three broken toes, a limp and advanced constipation. He staggered, muttered a few obscenities and collapsed in a final wave of exhaustion, dropping his prize beside him. The sack

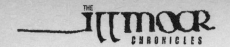

wriggled as it hit the floor, and continued to do so for several minutes. Then it seemed to give up. The rest of the glade was still, with only the thief's heaving chest and slow, determined breaths punctuating the silence.

Time passed . . .

Presently, a barrowbird flew into the glade, landing on the gnarled lower branches of an ancient oak. It put its head on one side and considered the scene.

The thief, whose distinguishing features included one mechanical arm and a moon-shaped scar dissecting his chin, struggled to raise a charred eyebrow. The commotion inside the sack had started up again, and even appeared to be building; yet he took no notice.

Still, the bird watched.

A few minutes later, the thief had taken to rolling around on the grass in a number of failed attempts to get to his feet. Finally, he made a desperate lunge at the oak, twisted around and shouldered himself up. Blood rushed in his head as he fought to maintain his balance.

The barrowbird, totally nonplussed by the sudden display of energy, fixed its beady eye on the sack.

Grinswood had become eerily silent. Shadows

merged, and the trees seemed to move with them.

The thief took one last look around.

'Time to move,' he muttered, snatching up the sack and urging himself into a run.

When he'd disappeared from view, the barrowbird twitched and ruffled its feathers. Then it flew up on to a higher branch and cast a glance down the forest path, where a trail of disturbed foliage marked the thief's progress.

I'll take my time, it thought, *this one looks like he's come a long way.*